PEACOCK
MORNING

Hilde Knorr

*To the people
of my life's landscape,
all of whom have given me
something of their own lives,
I dedicate this book.*

*It is the kind of novel often
called fact/fiction, but the fictions
are as true, in their own way,
as the facts. They have simply
been experienced, like music,
on a more receptive level.*

PEACOCK MORNING

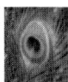

HILDE KNORR

David Lovell Publishing
Melbourne Australia

First published in 1998 by
David Lovell Publishing
PO Box 822
Ringwood Victoria 3134
Australia
Tel +61 3 9879 1433
Fax +61 3 9879 1348

Cover design by Creative Times, Richmond
Design by David Lovell
Typeset in 12.2/15 Adobe Garamond
Printed & bound in Australia by Imprenta P/L

National Library of Australia
Cataloguing-in-Publication data

Knörr, Hilde, 1920– .
  Peacock morning.
  ISBN 1 86355 065 8.
  I. Title.
A823.3

Contents

To be creative is to be part of the self-organizing process of the ongoing universe. It is to cooperate in shaping matter and energy in order to move towards a higher plane of existence.

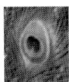

CHAPTER ONE

House with Birds

I COME FROM THE DIRECTION of the mountain and I approach the house as one deeply familiar with it.

Like the mountain it is enthroned in wide countryside without ostentation. It belongs to the homestead of an original squatter's run, and was placed here to pay homage to all the visible alpine chain in the east, and to my mountain in particular.

To all windows of its many rooms the landscape presents facets of its vast sky and restless clouds, its slopes and flowing rivers, its pattern of meadows and cultivation, and its moving cattle and shadows. Most of the other human habitations are screened off by trees, or the folds of nearer hills, so the mountain with its changing moods and colours is easily central to vision. On its slopes outcrops of rock make light or dark patches, often so deep as to suggest mysterious caves, or lurking entrances to hidden clefts and secret valleys.

This is what we saw reflected, piece by piece,

in the staring uncurtained windows of the house, when we first came upon it.

It was a big house for the old pioneering days when it was built, and it is evident that its architect sought to adapt the building experience of the old world to the new so as to regulate the home environment from a disposition to excessive heat rather than to warm it up against outside cold. It was erected when only people with extensive land holdings built large country dwellings. Its size and age are enough to invite speculation as to the manner of its building, and curiosity as to the history which has been absorbed by its walls.

Something of that history is visibly recorded in the materials of which it is built, and in the evidence of hands since laid upon it. At times it has suffered from those hands, and at others been blessed by them. Because it was built with integrity and purpose it has been only slowly moving towards dissolution.

Because of all this we, a sculptor and a writer, were in deep sympathy with it from first sight. Even before it came to be for sale, we were enthralled by its landscape, its historical significance, and the possibility of important understandings and fulfilments.

On a July day in 1978 when the sky seemed so low as to be just above the eyebrows, Daniel and I came to it from the auction in which we had been the final bidders. With us we brought the elation and trepidation which must always accompany those who have acquired a property against what seems to be good sense, good advice and good arithmetic, simply because of an inner conviction that it should be so.

We had previously inspected it well enough to realize that a different light might flow between us in this first encounter since responsibility had been added to dream.

The weak winter sun was behind the western hills as we drove across the river and saw that the mountain range to the east was coloured in violet, rose and indigo, while the west was lit by only fading gold.

We stopped the car at the gate and looked up the hill to where the house sits in beautiful harmony, with its stables and a dozen wonderfully-spreading river redgums outlined clearly against the slope behind. In that late light the wider background of near hills were vaguely seen as steeply rising and thickly forested.

Because we were now possessed by the tribal urge to feel our own land beneath our feet we left the car and walked. It must have been very cold, because I remember Daniel taking off his warm scarf and winding it around my head and neck. 'I'll have to teach you how to keep up your body heat in snow country', he said while he zipped his woollen jacket closer to his own more rugged form, and pulled his beret down over his ears.

As we went, hand in hand, we automatically settled ourselves into the landscape by halting every few metres and turning to view it from a new elevation. The evening was fading quickly and the sight did not range far.

As we approached the house, thin, foggy rain began to fall, fading out the glory of the golden light, darkening the granite steps and pearling the bare branches of two huge walnut trees on the far side. It was such fine moisture that the drifting veils of mist formed themselves into phantom shapes moving as though to enter the buildings which stood so deeply remote in their own winter pool of quietness.

The sight of them took Daniel back to the culture of his youth. 'Those mist-shapes — they are coming like the Earl King's daughters', he said, with a shiver. 'The Schubert song has suddenly become real!' He sang a seductive line or two softly, before adding, 'I wonder what can be waiting for us here? I know it's only an old superstition*, but please stay close to me.'

I can now empathize with those evocative forms far more than I could then. Looking back, I see them

* German folklore. The Earl King and his daughters lie in wait in the fog to lure travellers to their Kingdom of Death.

4

as welcoming beings rather than eerily-blown shapes of mist. Whichever they were that evening, it was some comfort when we were no longer in direct contact with them, and were able to feel the protection of the front verandahs about us, and their dry boards beneath our feet.

Those verandahs are wide, high off the ground and balustraded by sections of vertical cast iron lacework standing a few centimetres apart. On the west side some were missing or broken. Prior rain had soaked the thick flooring to a distance of a metre from the edge, and to that point the boards, running lengthwise, had, some time this century, been replaced. The rest were the originals, with the heads of handmade nails slightly protruding. Above us the underside of an estimated seventy-seven hundred yellow box shingles showed us part of the excellent condition of the whole of the original shingled roof of the house, covered in later years by galvanized iron.

Many years and experiences further on, I remember the length of the verandah and the lovely rising of the mountain in the east. Where there now stands comfortable and elegant furniture, there was one simple stool, long enough to seat ten people, but worn and battered enough for the previous owners to have thought it not worth removing.

It was whole enough for us to seat ourselves for

a while, and to watch the continuing drift of fine rain before making our way around on to the side verandah.

Where it made a curve we faced one small room whose door stood open to show an ancient iron bedstead with sagging wire mattress. Not unaffected by thoughts of coming restoration, we then walked through an even smaller room, with an old-fashioned, chain-operated toilet, to emerge on the more sheltered back verandahs.

These protect the walls facing the courtyard formed by two wings. Here only the cellar entrance is cast iron enclosed, and the floors are of brick, sloping gently down to ground level where they end in wide gutters of the same material.

The kikuyu grass of the raised lawn of the courtyard was then as yellow as daffodils. Irregular patches of the river-worn stones, which were part of the original cobbles it had been sown to cover, showed at its winter-worn edges.

Every single thing stood out with a detail it had never managed during our pre-sale inspections.

Over on the right, water from the verandah roof was beginning to dribble into a solitary, rust-streaked tank, drawing attention to lines of sagging and gaping guttering and rusty downpiping. Ten scaly doors — on the other side of whose interesting doorknobs were histories soon to reappear —

presented themselves directly to the courtyard and to us.

Beyond the knobbly, winter-bare grape vines, which grew in three clumps between eastside and westside verandahs, a spread of choughs, most family-conscious of ravens, walked companionably and diagonally across to where a giant elm tree held out its great, bare branches. The nearby stable building looked down from its slight eminence. Its sagging and gaping doors and windows emphasized the seriousness of the commitment we had recently made.

I remember waiting for Daniel to say judicially: 'Well, we've certainly bought ourselves a load of work! Do you really think you'll be equal to it, Gillian, old girl?' But his mind had evidently retained the romance which had seemed to emanate from the previously sunshine-clad building.

'Peacocks! Peacocks!' he cried, excitedly. 'It needs peacocks! Don't you think it has been made for peacocks?'

That was when the universe first presented the birds to us. They were there before they were born — becoming solidly vivid to our senses though not yet communicated to them by our eyes. Their brilliance flashed across the dull grey evening, brightening the courtyard, lighting the sky of our future! They were set moving in our minds years before they made their evening and morning walks along the verandah rails; they were present long before they began to spend long hours watching Daniel while he worked, and inspiring him to create a flowing sculpture* on the basis of the innate simplicity which lay beneath the gorgeous plumage.

They are gone from Jinwirringee and from us, but now that Time's length has been shortened by broader perspectives, they are as present as when they were spoken of on that first July day.

* Called 'Peacock Morning' and now in the Bright Art Gallery, Victoria.

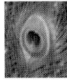

CHAPTER TWO

Shades and Shadows

PEACOCKS THERE MAY HAVE been before our time, or even many intervals of peacocks, but when we come to Jinwirringee to live, they are only thoughts lost among the historic shades we daily encounter in our new surroundings.

On the near edge of the dimly seen crowd are naturally those associated with what our eyes can see clearly. They are those who designed the house to have high ceilings, service wings, sunken cool rooms and a deep dry cellar. They are those who worked granite for the foundations and the steps, who made bricks, cut down trees, built walls, shingled roofs and laid floors.

Their faces are misty and their forms make no approach to us, for time and effort are no longer their preoccupations. Yet we are able to sense their wistful regret that the house appears as it does, and to feel that if we pay attention to them we will be shown how to restore it to life. We also feel a sense of urgency, as though they are pleading the dedicated service of hearts and hands to save their original thoughts from death or mediocrity.

When we have been inhabitants for a little longer, other faces sit around worn fireplaces or move among the furniture. There come to be fainter, rougher hands and forms — uniformed figures not included in family photographs, but performing duties in house and meat room and dairy. Stronger arms draw water from the twenty-metre deep and very narrow well, lined with stone and probably Chinese built, which we have soon discovered under the grass covering the cobbled courtyard.

Other shades begin to move in with the renewing of the garden: the people who worked, or merely walked and thought small thoughts or great amongst the inspiration of trees and flowers and vegetables. Even more become visible as we learn where other outbuildings, such as bakery and smithy once stood; and more still as we became familiar with the various divisions of the stable building. We move with a consciousness of the house's memory of veritable graveyards full of lives.

Over and above all we never lose the feeling of reciprocal relationship between buildings, land and mountain.

The stables and the trees are Daniel's expressed reason for being here, although, like myself, he is too romantic to have fully investigated their needs before committing himself.

Having done his part in making the main house liveable, pending further understanding of its needs, he commits himself to making the stables suitable for his own.

The lower storey of the building is of hewn granite blocks, and the floors cobbled with river stones like those of the courtyard, but the lofts, which run the entire length, are of brick. At the back, the mortar of the mid-nineteenth century being weak, this section is sagging outwards in the middle. Here Daniel, before we came to the house to live, began to build four heavy buttresses from stone and brick. It is typical of a sculptor that he finds it hard to repeat himself, and each of them is somewhat different from its predecessor.

After much thought we decided to pull down the crumbling and dangerous wall dividing the stablehands' sleeping quarters from the main lofts, and to turn the upper storey into a long display studio for all sculptures present and to come. The event is vivid in memory now, not only for the joy of discovering the basic symmetry of the loft's shape, but for the amount of work I carried out in loading the bricks into the wheelbarrows — and for the great crashes they made when Daniel wheeled them to the cat-head and tipped them out on to the ground below.

It was somewhere around this time that the

events of the past began to translate themselves into poems I must write. I welcomed the ideas with a full heart for I had already begun to dread that the physical demands of restoration would swallow inspiration, and I would never write again. But under the influence of the idea our actions became very allied with past happenings, the song of the magpies to vibrate through birds of other centuries.

> *Both dead and living are the hands*
> *that scrape and fill the stable bricks*
> *or match the fractured marble*
> *lying on some Hellenistic hill.*
> *The magpie and the nightingale*
> *that sang them through the centuries*
> *have never met at all*
> *but sing together still.*

Vivid, too, is another memory of singing sound — this one experienced with our first windstorm at the homestead. It was nothing like the familiar, gustily breathing winds which blew around our former home in the Dandenong Ranges. There they come through many kilometres of tall, straight trees whose lower leaves are often twenty metres above the ground.

That night, at Jinwirringee, our comprehension of storm was intensified because we were sleeping close to bare floors in empty rooms and thus, although each wall of the house sits on solid granite foundations, we received ground noises more clearly. Four metres overhead, the tongue-and-groove pine ceilings were no barrier to all the unnatural sounds produced by the hills and valleys of the roof. Myriad voices of the wind screamed and shrieked around it and sucked and strained and heaved at it the long night through.

Add to this the voices of cattle, close up to the house because not yet fenced off from it, and now in a very disturbed state. In the great orchestra of sound, a bull, or bulls, took the parts just above the thunder, while the more strained voices of cows mingled fittingly with the intensity of the winds. I could feel for the beasts. They were not enclosed by walls of triple brick; the trees which usually gave them friendly shelter had become a mass of whirling threats.

My own fear was so mixed with exultation in the effects produced that I felt in danger of becoming so identified with the storm as to will myself to be sucked up the chimney and out into the maelstrom of the night in order to be whirled around and around in ascending spirals with leaves and branches and loose pieces of buildings until I was forced into the very eye of the storm. Would there be breath enough for me? Or was there, in that place so mysteriously known as an eye, only a vacuum maintained by the force of the storm? Or was it the vacuum which caused the rushing of the whirlwind?

I had learnt that the sun is the 'engine' that drives the weather, but not too much more. Thought of the lack of knowledge eclipsed the storm for a few moments. I picked up the torch which lay beside our mattress and slipped out from under the covers to get to my feet and write a reminder note to find out more.

Even in the row going on around us my move more or less woke Daniel. 'What now? What can be the matter? Are you worried, dear? You don't need to be. The wind is only being dramatic. I'll guarantee it can't do anything to this house — it's as solid as a castle. It isn't at the storms' mercy, like a ship at sea — it stands for another couple of hundred years.' He was almost asleep again, but held himself back to offer a little advice. 'It's the sound which frightens — like in a battle. A pillow over the head is good for keeping out noise. Just relax and go back to sleep.'

He slumbered on the word, but I had already been reassured by the voice and the memory of it being just as positive during such a storm in Bass Strait. He was right! It was really nothing here where the walls did not rise and fall, nor creak as though they would be ripped apart; neither did all the free liquids in the body fight for liberation.

We emerged together into the washed sunlight of the new day to find that the windstorm had been at work, despite Daniel's assurances, on both house and stable, and even on elm trees close by. There the cattle, their night of terror forgotten, were calmly sampling the leaves of fallen boughs. Ourselves, looking around, assessed the future a little less optimistically, not knowing that such violence, though occasionally uprooting even giant trees, or ripping off a few roofs, is fairly rare in this district.

Apart from making a lot of scattered debris, this storm had been so playful with our own roofs as to twist and crumple the ridging of both the east wing and the stables. The galvanized iron at the very top was now so curled as to have an appearance as insubstantial as those paper spills which, in the old days, were used to carry fire from hearth to pipe or candle or lamp.

We were sharply reminded of the dedication needed for owning a nest for all seasons, a hopefully inviolate resting place, and above all a refuge from the searching eyes of our own kind who, even now, were moving to inspect our discomfiture.

Every other form of moving life may look at us as it will. We read no contempt in the eyes of worm or insect, bird or beast. We think of ourselves as being to them the lordly creatures who are able to change ourselves and the formation of the world.

15

We feel that they must have realized, by this time, that power of humans which may be looked upon, begged from, or cooperated with, but never challenged without hurt. Because of this comparative helplessness, it is easy to forget that they are fully capable of satisfying their own needs, even if, like the birds, those needs made them take yearly world journeys long before any person was known to have circumnavigated the globe. They were selecting materials for building with regard to qualities and ability to hold contours, were using those materials intricately, and furnishing and decorating their homes long before humankind ever got the idea. And as to adapting themselves to the evolution of the earth, we seem to be aeons behind.

Occasionally, some of what the independent animals really think of us manages to get through. While we were repairing the storm damage, Daniel blocked up a piece of pipe which swallows were using as a way into the roof of the stables. They assaulted him on the ladder, they followed him down the slope telling him what they thought of him in abusive bird dialect, and using the utmost violence of their beaks and claws until, with hands submissively over his head, he escaped into his own inviolate nest.

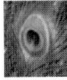

CHAPTER THREE

Adam

AT THIS POINT IN MY narrative I must stop and make sure of my direction. This could so easily become another book about the homestead and how it was restored, or about other parts of our lives, near and far. Our wonderful friendships, our family joys, troubles, achievements and crises are to be imagined as going on with unabated vigour and loyalty all the time we were at Jinwirringee. This story is very selective because it is about those events, those changes to our hearts and minds which the mingled experiences of the place and ourselves brought into the light.

As I look for the threads which will lead me to understand those happenings, I find myself going back in time to Hume and Hovell, the first white men recorded as having crossed the Murray River near Albury, and surveyed the countryside.

They found the land very beautiful, the timber of a most valuable kind, and wild flax growing to perfection. They described the native people as numerous, but rarely seen, and also wrote of them as being not aggressive, and very quick to pick up the meaning of the spoken word.

But Hume and Hovell were not looking for land for their own personal possession, nor were they destroying the wildlife food of the owners and substituting cattle and sheep which could not be hunted.

It is the squatter of a few years later who takes up the weapons of personal violence when the new food is perceived as a rightful replacement for what has been taken away. For the newcomer, reared in the commercial world, all things which stood in the way of acquisition must be got rid of — they being fairly sure, by Britannia's own example, that not even her justice will stand up for those who can show no visible Title to Land.

Both sides of the resulting conflict were represented in the man who was moving towards us. Even though he was tall, strong and handsome, his colour proclaimed him one of those whose every aspect will always in some sense dispute the rightfulness of our own title. We had taken possession of the homestead those first title holders built, and were in that state of sympathy which is a precursor to becoming a part, known or forgotten, of its future history.

We had finished clearing the debris of the storm, and were putting down roots by planting trees and listening to the morning chorus of birds when

Adam completed his journey to us with dew on his hair, and twigs and grass on his damp clothes. He was, we saw, not much more than thirty years old, clean, gaunt and hungry.

He asked for work. I knew instantly that Daniel would employ him without question, for Daniel had not only a keen interest in history, but a sensitivity to those who have been wronged. In South Africa he had also experienced their woes from a similar disadvantaged situation. Now here was one in a different country but like circumstances, asking for help. He felt complimented and invigorated by the plea, like a knight called to rescue. His very first question was not as to what Adam could do, but what we could do for him.

So he was brought inside and set down to consume the largest breakfast I have ever seen eaten, while we had our usual bowl of porridge.

Now, once again unsure of myself, I look back to ruefully ask my memory whether or not I would have been so acquiescent if it had been set plainly before me that I would be expected to occupy many hours of my already well-filled life in preparing three such substantial meals every day, with regular morning and afternoon teas thrown in. I ask myself whether, in the long run, this simple, daily exigency could have influenced me in the decisions I was later called to make.

Certainly it increased my fears that the magnitude of what we were attempting would make deeper incursions into my time rather than that of Daniel. I had thought, in fact we had discussed, how good it would be, after all the years of mothering and fathering, to no longer feel that parenting should have priority over all else. We had no place in our programme for a resident not only almost young enough to be another involving child, but one who could be said to have as much or more of an historical claim upon us.

Adam was intelligent. He made poetry and read books. It was a pleasure to lend him what we had, the kind of almost boastful pleasure every owner of well-stocked bookshelves feels when called to provide more than the daily newspaper or a magazine. More so because Adam had come to us without even a swag.

We found we could often have good discussions with him, but it soon became apparent that some areas had dangerous borders. As he became freer with us we began to sense a deeply subjective, almost suspicious scrutiny of all that we said, as if all our sentences could hold subtle undertones of contempt for the black man.

But later, as the weeks went by, and he felt he was appreciated, he appeared to become more relaxed.

Nothing about Adam seemed to feel strange to Daniel. Neither was he, who was such a work fanatic, in the least concerned when Adam would sometimes let himself be still for minutes on end just to watch things. We both soon saw that Adam's way of watching any natural phenomena was different from ours. For us, as for most of our race, Nature was superb, enchanting, delightful — or some such adjectives — but we, even though we belonged to it, were something set apart by feeling ourselves to be at the apex of all things. For Adam it was a relationship in which neither comparisons nor words were needed: there was no dividing duality in it.

As the weeks went on we had better and better conversations. We discussed several books in depth, including my book, *The Mystic Lake*, published the year before. He said he had never read another Australian book which was like it, and that I had the beginnings of real perception.

Daniel was so pleased with this that he read him a poem I had just written, but was so enthusiastic himself that he didn't leave Adam any room to manoeuvre.

One evening Adam spoke of it, and then referred to the extraordinary senses of the Aborigines, whom he thought of as predominant in his genes, and therefore his people. He felt this was right because their heritage was in a past far deeper than that of the intruding whites. He asserted that not only has the Aborigine not lost relationship to the external world in the way that city-dwellers and white ants have done, but, as well as retaining the power to communicate without words, has remained open to the whole universe, thus understanding how to move around in it without being perceptibly absent from earth. Which was why the achievements of the white people meant so little to them; they had seen wonders beyond the white dream. While the rest of the world had concentrated on possessions, the Aboriginal people had explored the powers of the spirit — powers which were regarded with grave mistrust by even the monks of the monastery of Subiaco in Western Australia, who he thought should have known better.

He told us his mother had left him with them when he was about nine years old. She told the Brothers and Fathers she brought him to be taught as a white boy because the blacks had no more part in this world. Adam remembered her as very thin and ill, and some days not able to walk, or even to talk, because of continuous coughing. He spoke huskily of those memories, struggling with the tight cobweb bonds of childhood. The monks were not unkind. They taught their charges many things, but this one was old enough to find the most emphatic 'truths' totally foreign. When he learned to read the Bible it was better, because much of it was told in the same way as Aboriginal myth.

He had nothing very bad to say of the Benedictines. They fed and clothed, as well as taught. They laughed and played games, and fished and worked with the boys, but it was all in white man's way. All the time he hoped and prayed his mother would return for him. He wanted her to be pleased because he was trying so hard to learn what the white people knew, while remaining a dark person so he could be one with her. Every time Aborigines came to the monastery, he was in a fever of hope. Though he was often able to make talk with and sometimes to question the travellers, he never saw or heard of his mother again.

When he left the place at fifteen he began his search for her, and for his own people. But, although he would have been willingly received by several of the tribes, he didn't find one to whom he felt related. It was almost sure that his mother was dead, and very possible that her close kinspeople no longer existed. He knew that he had also probably lost his ability to belong, but no amount of reasoning was able to keep him from continuing the search up and down the land, not drawn by the songlines, but still compelled from within.

He had married and had children, but now they

also were not for him. He was the foreign one who wasn't even able to relate to his own family. Once, in jail, a psychiatrist had told him that this was because of his resentment against his broken relationship with his mother. But part of it was due to alcohol.

On the last word he was suddenly, almost fierily accusing. He knew we had suspected him already. What else would have made us hide our alcohol away and never drink when he was there? We might think we were enlightened, but we were infected with the white-man belief that all blacks are alcoholics. He added that the white man doesn't like to see the black man drinking — it's a mirror of himself if he had the same social structure, the same underdog status. Before we could attempt to discuss what he said he got up and left the room.

It took him some time to get back to his previous ease with us, and then he took care to warn us further. He told how he had once been released from jail on condition that he become a member of Alcoholics Anonymous. He said that he was a foreigner there, too, but had tried hard to see himself as a brother to the other sufferers instead of a victim. He could sometimes stay off the grog for weeks, but downfall after downfall made his struggles seem to be of no use at all. He gave up, and from then on his bouts were deeper and almost invariably landed him in jail. He added savagely that we could kick him out if we liked. It wouldn't mean much to him. After all, he'd already been warned out of towns without number, and nearly every state of Australia.

Daniel almost choked with indignation at the last phrase. He didn't think such a thing could have happened to a white man. He assured Adam that he would be all right as long as he stayed with us; we would protect him whatever happened.

Daniel told me afterwards that it was our duty to keep Adam as long as possible.

I said that was all very well, but we didn't have money enough to spend on someone who was without the skills that we needed from now on. Daniel replied that that was how the squatters treated the Aborigines — just use them up to do the menial jobs and then chase them off! Adam was learning as fast as he could be taught. And then, reading my thoughts, 'Yes, I know it's a lot for you to do — having to produce his three enormous meals every day. But stick to it for a while longer, if you can'. And adding with true married guile, 'If I don't have to do all the odd jobs around the workshop myself, I'll have more time to help you with the restoring. If you think you're too much on your own you could join us and begin the things you've talked of doing to the studio'.

So I sometimes did that, but even though I was

accustomed to taking part in workshop activities, I was always the third person. We were two collaborating men and one only woman all the time.

It was at this time that Daniel, very sensibly, began to take Adam out fairly often into more remote areas to help him bring in red gum and red box logs from trees which had blown down, or been felled beside the roads and left lying for years and years. They were mostly well dried and ready for sculpting. The two men together could manoeuvre them on to the trailer and bring them home behind the Volkswagen Kombi van.

Bringing in the wonderfully grained wood made rich days for Daniel. When he returned from these forays his face would be glowing with such visions of what he could sculpt that he was already partly identified with the sculptures long before they even had a shape for him.

There was also another sort of identification growing in him. It came from Adam and his different way of relating to objective reality. Out in the open, with just another male for company, Adam was himself. He would explain how and why the hills and valleys had assumed their shapes, why this one would have been used for ceremonies, why that would have been avoided, why the songlines took the wanderers the ways they habitually went, or why ritual was important.

All of this was, of course, 'men's business' and could never be relayed to me. But it was important to me. It was the first time in nearly thirty years that Daniel had had a peculiar interest in any person other than myself and the family. Friends he had in plenty, loving and loved, but they were all shared with me in the home. I tell you this because I was conscious that there was now something that he could not share; and I really do not know how much this consciousness influenced me a little later on.

So weeks passed without Adam going into town by himself or having an alcoholic drink. It was a strange life for a man in his prime.

He went into the town with me one day. I must admit that I worried in case he should go to the hotel, but, as far as I knew, he did nothing other than take his sports jacket to the dry-cleaner — he was a fanatically clean fellow — and buy himself a paper to read while he sat in the car waiting for me to finish shopping. We were very pleased with his restraint. But there was a circumstance operating beyond our influence.

At the evening meal Adam was withdrawn, not asking for even one more helping, returning taciturn answers to Daniel's attempts at conversation. At last, when questioned directly if he was offended, he said he had seen other Aborigines in the town — a poor, dreary-looking group, like himself belonging nowhere. Yet they could be valuable if they were allowed.

Daniel said earnestly that there were thousands and thousands, even millions of whites, in similar bad circumstances, who felt just like that about themselves. He had learned in South Africa that people of any colour were the same when it came to living in poverty. Didn't Adam think that they all contributed something to what you might call the 'world-soul', the Great Spirit whom the Aborigines reverenced? He quoted the poet Robert Frost, because Adam had been reading my copy of his poems. *Men work together ... whether they work together, or apart.* 'Never fear, Adam, the Aboriginal people of Australia will still influence the world!'

But Adam clearly would have none of it. He went off to his room, which was in the east wing. For days his humour was up and down. One night, at about ten o'clock, he came in to our bedroom to demand his pay and a ride into town.

Very fraternally, Daniel tried to argue him out of it. He asked why Adam wanted to go at night. He couldn't get transport till the morning, and he wouldn't get a bed at this late hour.

Adam said he was well aware that, as a blackfellow, he would get neither, but for the same reason it was quite natural for him to sleep under the stars. 'The taxi won't refuse my money in daylight.'

Daniel persisted. 'Go to bed, Adam, and have a good rest. If you still want it, I'll fix up everything early tomorrow, and I'll take you to where you want to go.'

Adam turned away, but swung on his heel to say passionately, 'You are so blind! You're probably blaming me for being ungrateful, but I tell you I can't go on suffering like this — not even for you. I can't go on living every day in this house with them under my feet — moving in the walls — in the air — black men and women — girls who served the whites or died. I can't go on walking with booted feet every day on this ground, consenting with my body to all the things that were done in this countryside — with your kindness — your bloody kindness — undoing me! I've got to get out!'

I had a vision of how we must present to him — a married couple of the present ruling class, dressed for the night, sitting propped up with soft pillows in an antique cedar bed with a bellrope on each side to call slaves such as himself. I was unable to find consoling words.

Daniel still reached out. 'Can't you let it die between us? Just between *us*, Adam? It would be a start.' He swung his feet out and sat on the edge of the bed. 'Adam, you'll never be free of resentment about the past until you concentrate on what you can do with the present. I know! I know! I've been through it all, as a long term prisoner-of-war, as a displaced person.'

But Adam literally hurled himself away and was out in the passage before the sentence was complete. A moment later we saw his shadow cross the window blind in as tragic a mime as ever screen showed.

Daniel went after him, and didn't come back for what seemed a long time.

'It's no good. I can't persuade him. He really wants to go', he told me as he got back into bed. 'I tried to get him to be positive about the position of the Aborigines, but I don't think he really listened. I couldn't say as much as I wanted to, because I know I can't give all of myself to becoming involved with him. And he knows as well as we do that there's really nothing for him in this district, no matter how hard he tries. He's in his prime and living like an ascetic — which I know he's not. And he knows we're only keeping him on out of sympathy.

'Now I've accepted that he's got a right to do what he wishes without argument, I just want him to get away without spoiling the time he's had with us. I've told him we want him to be able to come back and share with us again. I've done everything I can do. I've settled his wages, and promised to drive him to the railhead in the morning. Perhaps by then he'll have himself in hand.'

The sun woke us in the morning. Our orange

30

cat was reaching a paw through the space under the partly-opened sash window as though he would catch us and draw us out into the good day. His demand for breakfast was suddenly lost in a much more fearsome sound coming from where Adam slept in the east wing.

He was declaiming from the Bible in the manner of a hell-fire preacher. Like any such, the words belonged neither to love nor to the peaceful morning. *Therefore the sword shall never depart from thy house, for thou hast despised me.* The voice sank, then rose again more ominously, *Behold, I will raise up evil against thee … I will take thy wives before thine eyes!*

I was appalled. 'Daniel! He's gone mad!'

'No, he's not mad, but he is very drunk!' replied Daniel grimly. 'That's the way it takes people like him. I'll bet he's been at our wine — I didn't shift it after he spoke about us hiding it because I thought it might be good to show that we trusted him. Well, I suppose I must get dressed and be prepared for trouble.'

I was out of bed and into my jeans and shirt before his feet had touched the floor.

He stared. 'Aren't you having a shower?'

'And maybe get caught while you're getting dressed! You know there's not a lock on any door.'

He said not to be so jumpy — no wonder no

scrap of fat ever clung to me. He was sure Adam hadn't been meaning me when he talked about taking wives. He was only expressing the intensity of his emotions. And it was good that he was reading from the Bible, wasn't it?

I wasn't so sure of that, and I was very aware that the glimpses of drunkenness which were all that had entered my life had never held a threat like this.

Underneath our own dialogue we had still been able to hear Adam reading, but now he must have found a passage which suited his mood for his voice grew stronger, softened again, and then grew suddenly louder, throbbing its way menacingly through the window.

And bringing forth the people of the city, he sawed them, and drove over them with chariots of iron, and divided them with knives, and made them to pass through brick kilns.

'That can't be the Bible!' I cried in horror.

'It is,' Daniel replied sardonically. 'It's about the *perfect man after God's own heart* — King David — in his less amorous moments, acting for the good of his people.'

We went to where we had hidden the wine. At least half of it was gone. Its absence also showed us that Adam had been poking around the house. I, at least, felt territorially affronted as we went together to the kitchen to put the kettle on. 'What will we do if he comes in for his early coffee? How long will it take to wear off? Who could we get to help?'

Daniel looked at me with gratitude and I knew he was as worried as myself. 'Well, why don't we take a cue from what he's told us, and from his present behaviour, and try to get a priest, or someone like that? One of them might know which part of the Bible to read to pacify him.'

So I went to the phone and tried and tried before hurrying back. 'The priest is saying Mass. One minister wasn't answering. The other had gone out to a very ill parishioner, but his wife told me the number of a local doctor who works with Alcoholics Anonymous. He also had to go out urgently, but he'll come as soon as he can. In the meantime, if Adam should become violent I must ring the police immediately.'

'No! No police! No! I think I can manage. First, let's see if he'll come and have some black coffee.'

'Not in here!' I cried, with visions of being chased from room to room. 'We'll have it out on the verandah.'

Daniel actually laughed. 'Don't look so scared! He's only drunk. And I think we could both run faster than he could at this moment, even at our age.'

I had just put the coffee tray down on the verandah table when Adam appeared in his doorway. He stood there for a minute or two, swaying like a dark pendulum against the light of the window behind. Great swags of glistening saliva hung from his mouth and chin, and swung about as he moved forward. He didn't look like Adam. His features seemed all exaggerated. His eyes were great, dark-red wheels in his sagging face.

'You look bloody awful, Adam', called Daniel cheerfully when Adam was close enough. 'Come and sit down, and have a couple of coffees to sober you up.'

'Are you calling me drunk, you white bastard?' asked Adam companionably, as he made his difficult way toward us. He managed to seat himself on a stool, and Daniel helped him to get a hold on the coffee mug. He sat there with his back to the daylight, trying to sip the liquid while the saliva maintained its steady flow and settled on the mug and his hands.

I was revolted, and went to the nearby herb patch and began to dig the friendly earth.

I heard Adam speak to Daniel, but the words were blurred. Then I heard strong anger in Daniel's reply. Afterwards he told me that what Adam had said referred to what he would very much like to do to me. Daniel had ordered him to go and have a long, cold shower.

'Whiteys think they can wash everything off

with soap', replied Adam ponderously, but clearly. He managed to attain a roughly vertical stance. 'Got to have private word', he said and began to orient himself in my direction.

Daniel gripped his arm. 'You do what I say, and do it now! Go and have a cold shower!' Adam went a few paces towards the bathroom, but turned back towards his bedroom.

Daniel had taken the coffee mugs into the kitchen and returned (I think to keep watch over me) before Adam came out on to the verandah again. This time he had a bottle in his hand. He went to Daniel and demanded a bottle-opener. Then his voice, endeavouring to be engaging, 'You have a drink with the black man?'

'No bottle-opener', replied Daniel. 'And no drink! I've eaten and drunk with you hundreds of times, and there's no need for me to do it when you've already had too much.' He reached out a hand for the bottle. 'Give that to me, and go at once and have that shower. Then we'll talk, if you want to.'

I remember thinking that he, who usually seemed rather timid, was really very brave when the situation called for it.

'You telling me what to do, you white bastard? You telling me when to knock off? Tell you what I'll do. When I finish this one, I'll finish you, too. Won't be the first whitey I've bashed, or the first white woman I've fixed up! Won't be the last!' He waved the bottle around in the air in drunken imitation of such a bashing, before moving to the nearby granite windowsill where, at the third attempt to coordinate, he knocked off the top of the bottle neatly against the lower edge. He waved his achievement victoriously at Daniel, poured a deep swig of the wine down his throat, and wobbled back to his stool.

I could see Daniel was angry. I went around the side of the house and came down the passage to the telephone. I meant to ring the doctor who worked with Alcoholics Anonymous — or I think I did. But as I raised the receiver there was a noise from the verandah.

Fearing that there might be violence, I looked out, but it was only that Adam had swayed a little far on his stool and finished up in the gutter, the bottle still in his hand. Daniel approached him with the obvious intention of helping him up, pleading with him, stretching out both of his hands.

I saw Adam change his grip to the neck of the bottle but, in my ignorance, I only thought he was meaning to retain it. He made as if to rise but, when his helper came near, he made a wild swing with his glass club, missing Daniel's head by very few millimetres.

Daniel retired quickly. For the first time, I could see he was shaken. He was also shocked, I think, to have received such treatment from his friend.

For me Adam was suddenly too much of a menace, too much trouble altogether. With the phone cord extended so I could keep a terrified eye on events I rang the police.

Then I picked up a broom which was the only weapon I could see, and ran down the passage and around the house to come upon Adam in the rear if necessary. On the corner I pulled up suddenly.

Daniel was over near the wall, looking at Adam. He was standing half-erect in the gutter, staring back, the bottle hanging loosely from his hand. As I watched, he, still looking intently at Daniel, turned it upside down and let the purple wine gurgle out to run away down the gutter. When the bottle was empty he threw it away over the lawn without looking where it fell. Of all the actions of that morning these are the ones which seem the most symbolic and have come to haunt me most.

Then Adam turned himself away from Daniel and went towards his room. He put his hand on the door, but moved away instead and stood looking down over the iron balustrade which protects the depths of the cellar.

I think he was waiting for a move from Daniel — one which would take him back to companionship and strength, but I don't know if I thought it then, or shortly afterwards.

At that moment I was concerned for Daniel,

because he had seated himself at the table and closed his eyes. He looked very shaken, and my fear for him grew, for he was five years older than I, and temperamentally unsuited for violence of any kind. Later I learned that he was only quieting his mind for what might happen next.

As I approached him I knew I had already negated any good that might have happened from Adam's action. Daniel looked up and smiled into my anxious face. 'It's going to be all right, old girl. Another cup of coffee might fix it all.'

It was very hard to bring out the words that would tell him how difficult it would be. I said, 'Not coffee, not anything! I don't think it can be fixed now. I saw Adam try to hit you. I was scared for you. I called the police. Shall I try to stop them?'

As I turned myself about to re-enter the passage which ran right through the house, I saw the police car turning to come into our drive. I turned back. 'They're coming now. The police are coming! I'm sorry!'

'You did what you thought was right', Daniel said sighing as he rose from the chair. 'But we'd better go and warn Adam.'

Then we saw that he had moved over to the main house and seated himself on the long form against the wall. We knew by his attitude that he had heard our words. He sat there, with his elbows on his knees and his face buried in his hands, while the police came across the grass he had mowed, and picked up the empty bottle on the way.

We had not met these policemen. Daniel introduced ourselves and our friend, Adam. I said I was sorry for having troubled them. I thought Adam would be all right now. It was just that I didn't know anything about drinkers, and I was scared.

Adam lifted his face and looked at me. He said, ironically, 'You're a real Aussie, aren't you?'

I think he meant that I didn't have the courage to take responsibility for what I'd done, but I'll never be sure. I saw him as I thought the police must be seeing him — not as the intelligent man we knew, but as a disgusting drunk with wild eyes and ragged hair, with saliva falling from his lips and chin, though not in the skeins it had made earlier.

The policeman were not unaccustomed to such sights and were friendly to him, in a way. They asked him where he came from, and how he came to be at Jinwirringee. He answered them not a word.

Daniel put in as many good words as he could find, telling them how Adam had come and asked for work, how well he had done it, about AA and how this was the first time he'd broken out. He said earnestly that we'd all come to be good friends in the weeks he had been with us. 'Sorry to have bothered you at all', he added, becoming very

39

man-to-man. 'Wife felt it was a bit too much when he started swinging the — ' He stopped abruptly, realizing that in the middle of the sentence his sympathy had switched from Adam to myself and made him less wary of his words.

The policemen looked from him to Adam and back to us, and we could see them assessing his aggression, and weighing it against our vulnerability.

'Not a good way to behave when these people have made a friend of you', said one to Adam. Adam looked back out of his great, blackened eyes, and shook his head.

I felt that behind those disadvantaging eyes he was now sober enough to be aware, and very vulnerable. Daniel had the same idea. He must have wanted to make him appear to be better. He took out his handkerchief, wiped Adam's face with it and ran his fingers through his hair to tidy him up. 'I think he'll be all right now', he said.

The senior officer was visibly softened. 'All right, then', he said to Adam. 'So you went on a binge. We picked up another of your lot in the park this morning. He got a bit aggressive, too, so we had to put him inside to sleep it off. Were you with him?'

For the first time Adam defended himself, but not without aggression, 'No! Drink on my own! Black men don't like me. I don't like whiteys.'

'All right! Skip it! So you brought it home here.'

Daniel's met Adam's gaze, clearly giving him permission to say what he would, but he was too proud to lie. He said, 'No. Stole it from where they hid it.'

'Oh, you did, did you?' This was more serious to a policeman. 'How many bottles?'

'Don't know — three — four — five. Finished now.'

'Well, let's have a look at your room, just in case you've still got some stowed away.'

He helped Adam to his feet and held his arm as they went. As we followed I was desperately hoping I wouldn't be responsible for putting Adam in gaol, but I knew I didn't want him around the place any more. I didn't want to ever see again such a look as the one he'd given me when he called me a 'good Aussie', or the looks which had passed between himself and Daniel while he poured the wine out.

When the officer opened the door of Adam's room, the stench hit us as hard as moving solids meeting. The officer pushed the door wide, and the other one walked across to the sash windows and hauled both open. By the time this was done the shock to the olfactory nerves was almost lost in visual dismay. The room, which Adam usually kept clean and tidy, was in total disarray, as though one temporarily beyond his mind's control had been confined there. A large pool of vomit lay on the floor with the open Bible resting in it. On the table was another such pool with pieces of broken bottle for decoration. In the centre of all was a neat group of a dozen wine bottles, nine of which were without corks.

I remember a small part of my brain thinking it all made up an abstract that someone might paint one day, but most of my mind was receiving a series of awful visions of the night which had been progressing while we slept so close by and so unprotected.

I pushed them away and wondered with what enormous effort of will Adam had called himself back to some kind of rationality in order to face us.

I want to leave my story there, with all blame resting on Adam, but I can't. I have to tell how the policemen changed completely. 'Get your things together!' the sergeant ordered Adam. To Daniel he said, 'He can't stay here. You must see what danger there is to your wife, let alone yourself. We'll take him in until he sobers up, and tomorrow we'll send him over the border on the express train.'

Adam went mad. 'Take him! Take him again! Send him express out of one more state! Give him nowhere on earth to go! Take all, all, all! White man takes everything from black man! Land! Women!

Children! Friends! Everything!' It was a giant scream of pain.

Daniel was the first to pull himself back to speech. He said the policemen needn't bother: we wouldn't be preferring any charges. He'd get Adam to clean up the mess, and then he'd take him to the railhead himself.

The elder officer answered. 'All right, just as you like. As long as he goes at once. We'd better wait here, just in case you get too soft.' To me the other one added quietly that they'd follow the van to see that Adam didn't break out again, and he'd warn other police stations to look out for him.

Daniel and both policemen stayed with Adam as he restored the room to some sort of order. Feeling myself to be very unwanted, I took myself away. But soon, even as far off as the herb patch, I could hear the same tremendous voice which had so shaken me in the morning begin to roar out until it became a wide unbroken stream carrying every kind of insult, every sort of obscenity and threat. If either the police or Daniel answered, their voices were too controlled for me to hear.

When Daniel emerged with Adam he had him by the arm and was carrying clean clothes and a towel. Adam was still ranting that we would all get our deserts for what we were doing to him. If it took a lifetime, or had to be after he was dead, we could be sure he would return. But he became quiet when he realized it was Daniel alone who was leading him to the shower.

Not long afterwards the police came from the east wing, each carrying a bucket of dirty water which he emptied down the gully trap. Then they went back to come out with an armful of things that Adam had acquired since he came to us. We rolled them up in the blanket and put a strap around. The policemen set themselves down on the long form and waited.

Daniel left the bathroom before Adam did, and came to me in the kitchen where I was making coffee. 'Good girl! But I'll take it out to them. You look as if you've had enough. Let the men manage now.' But, despite his words, I followed him.

There was just one more explosion from Adam. He felt his bundle and asked where his books were. He targeted the police again. 'They call the Aborigines bloody thieves, but they aren't the only ones!'

One of the officers laughed. 'Here, hold on! How were we to know you could read?'

Adam stood stock still. His look was one of utter despair. What had been expressed in his attitude before this was, however aggressive and insulting, at least full of life passionately felt. The man who at last walked slowly through the open door of what had been his room and took up the small pile of books we had given him, looked so dead as to amaze by his movements.

There were two other books as well as those I had written. One was a small, fine-leafed anthology of ancient poems translated from the Greek. I had given it to Adam because he loved it so, and because he could carry it easily in his pocket. The other was a collection of modern poems from South African native people, which pleased him for a different reason. Now, thinking about these things, Daniel said to the officer who had last spoken. 'Not only can he read, but he can think like a scholar.'

Adam, with the books under his arm, came out of the room as if he neither thought nor heard. He walked slowly away along the brick verandah and out onto the drive.

None of us spoke or looked at each other until he would have reached the bottom of the slope and gone out of the gate. At last that same officer stirred, 'Hadn't we better do something? He looked as though he might do himself a mischief.'

I said, or it may have been wailed, 'Bring him back! Bring him back, and put him to bed. We'll look after him! He can go when he's better, if he must!'

Daniel said to me, 'No, no! He'll never come back now. Because you are a woman, and you've seen too much! He might have stood anything else.'

He picked up the swag which was still lying on the long seat. 'I'll see to him.' A minute after he left us we heard the engine of the Kombi come to life.

The policemen did, too. 'I suppose we'd better follow your husband', said the senior, pulling himself back to being a police officer. 'It's all very well being sorry for the abo, but you can't trust this type of drunk of whatever colour — one moment quiet as a lamb, the next violent. There's a lot of hate still to spill out of him. That's why they're safer in the lock-up.' He transferred his anxiety to me. 'You're sure you'll be all right? You'd better go and have a good lie down.'

Daniel came home two hours later with a face too full of pain for questioning, and with bolts for all the main doors and windows.

We were left in the kind of white possession enjoyed by all of the other people who have 'owned' Jinwirringee.

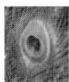

CHAPTER FOUR

The Promised Land

WE DID NOT HAVE TOWN water at Jinwirringee, but, as if to let us down lightly, the first two summers were blessed with ample rain and continuous growth. In the last month of the second season there was green all over, and still no fences to divide our two and a half hectares from the several hundred which had been sold at the auction.

Those few hundreds were a fraction of what the run had originally been, but for us it was a wide space gloriously unoccupied by other than ourselves and the wandering cattle. Many and many an early summer morning I roamed over its diversities — up the steep and timbered hills, down to where the rivers joined, over to where the biggest mine of the nine once working on the property still existed — always taking care, of course, that no uncharted shaft should catch me unaware, always cautious lest among the cattle, mostly polled, there might be a rampageous bull or two.

The lack of a fence dividing us off, the rare

visits of the owners, had this effect on me: I could climb to whatever vantage point I would, and survey the land as my own because I knew that only my eyes were seeing it from that place, that to no other in the world did it appear as it did to me. I was as Moses, or stout Cortez, or Christopher Columbus, none of whom would ever have title to the discovered land, but all of whom knew they had a kind of entail which would last much longer. Mine was not so permanent but I still had a contribution to offer and could descend to our own lovely scatter of buildings with it all wrapped in my heart.

There was a place not far from them, midway between the crests of hills, where there was a spring of fresh water. Below this spring was a dam where the cattle came to drink, and below that and over to one side was a well. To the right again the overflows from dam and well had made a seepage area of about half a hectare where a few pines grew and tussocks and bushes proliferated throughout the bog. Blackberries were interspersed in heavy clumps and grew in a thick hedge around more than half of the perimeter.

Very early one March morning, while the wonderful mists of autumn were still defining the lines of the rivers, and gently rising to the sun in the east, I went up to the seepage with a billy-can and a basket to pick the berries which showed among the leaves in inviting black clusters. Into this silent place, one of the many I already knew, I went without trepidation, for it appeared that all the cattle were far away and calmly grazing in the groupings which are their custom.

I was wrapped in joy at my lovely isolation and had picked the basket three parts full when there was suddenly a terrible crashing, as of some large body smashing and squelching its way towards me through the boggy undergrowth.

My mind ran fast through the terrors of it being a bull, a wild horse, a wild pig, or, more dreadful than all, some crazed creature of my own kind. The nearest to mad crazy I had ever seen was Adam drunk, Adam with drooling lips, Adam threatening Daniel with a bottle, Adam saying he would come back, whether dead or alive. The memory was still too close to be ignored. What if he had seen me leaving to come here and was fulfilling those dire threats of vengeance which neither Daniel nor I, after the first shock of hearing had worn off, had considered to be real. I don't think I really believed it now either, but a woman standing alone in an exposed position and hearing a frightening noise is very open to imagination.

My instinct was to remove myself to a safe place. Whatever the creature proved to be it was between me and the shelter of the pine trees — if shelter it could be called, because the jutting branches of those Australian cypresses have spiky wood, dead and alive, right from the ground up. They are almost impossible to climb, but may have made a screen.

The ten-foot-high blackberries behind me on the west side of the bog made an impregnable curve which cut off the north. To the south the bog was deeper, and there was too much of it.

There seemed to be only one thing to do, and I did it. I threw myself to the ground and rolled as far as I could under the overhanging canes of the blackberry bushes. Even as I did so I thought of my exposed basket and billy-can, and that my action could be the worst thing to have done if the crashing creature was human.

Only when I was fully in my hide, and as close to the thick canes as possible, did I think of the possibility of snakes being in there with me. Most snakes spent spring, summer and part of autumn on the lower slopes of the hills, on the flats and near the rivers, where many of them were killed by humans or automobiles. In late autumn they began to move up into the hills where they hibernated throughout winter. In the first winter we found that many had stopped en route and occupied the uninhabited parts of the homestead. We had been obliged to eject a number of them from wings and stables. Remembering all these things, only my need to be hidden from the unknown kept me for an instant where I was.

The revelation of that unknown's character took longer than I had expected. It was as if the thing beyond my sight was not coming in a straight line. It must be zig-zagging, or dodging something, although my ear to the ground told me it was coming ever closer. Soon I detected the accompaniment of a kind of grunting sound. What then could it be? The wild pig, if there was such a thing in this district, being chased by a dog? I immediately visualized the approaching dreadful creature as a boar with red eyes, ferocious teeth and fearsome tusks being forced ever closer to myself. The dog must be a very large one to take on such an antagonist. I saw the dog first as the rogue Alsation which had been harrying our neighbour's cattle; and then as one with an owner standing by to watch the antics taking place in the sticky marsh. On that thought I seemed to hear the short whistle with which a man calls his dog.

I did not need the sound of an even softer slither in the bushes behind me to make me come out of concealment. It was one thing to hide from an animal or a maniac. It was quite another to be discovered in such a humiliating position, first by the hunting instincts of the dog, and then by somebody who would recognize me and talk about it in the pubs, or at the local cattle sales. The slithering sound may have accelerated me a little, though it could well have been only a lizard.

I was standing up, noting how much I was bleeding from the sharp blackberry thorns while hastily brushing off dead scraps of wood and running fingers through hair, when the creature finally came into sight.

It was nothing more than a huge, harmless wombat — the largest I have ever seen. It was alternately up on its hind legs and down on all fours, forcing its clumsy body this way and that in order to escape the expert beak of an angry magpie.

Something happened to the morning, to all creation. I was no longer myself, in hiding, in a dilemma. Because of my flight into that hiding I was already the victim wombat. In the next moment, lifting the billy-can and hurling it at the magpie, I was the aggressor, and the bird, which was aggressive probably because of threatened territory, became the victim. By the time the wombat's dive, as precipitate as my own had been, had taken it deeply into the shelter of the blackberry hedge, the bird had soared and was back on track to the refuge of the nearest gum tree. I wondered if both bird and wombat were also glad no other of their kind had been there to witness.

I went down the shine of morning pondering

deeply over my sense of oneness and its relationship to corporate consciousness. It had not been difficult to be one with the wombat and all other creatures vulnerable, fearful and seeking sanctuary, but I found it hard to be one with the magpie aggressor. As soon as I tried to enter into that guilt my mind took the position of defender. It clung to the idea, as all territorians do, that it was only doing its duty — even though, as in the case of magpie, nation, religion, family — the territory has been arbitrarily marked off by itself. This, of course, included the original squatters; and it was just what I had begun to realize as a characteristic of myself. It was just what I had recently done to Adam.

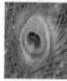

CHAPTER FIVE

The Coming of the Peacocks

TO BE GIVEN A GIFT OF peacocks is to become something else in stature, something elevated, or princely, or even pompous.

No spacious house, no capacious swimming pool with accompanying sauna, no pretentious and expensive motor car, could ever achieve the effect of a couple of peacocks in the right setting. A peacock emerging from a shrubbery, even when only trailing its tail, is a promise of display no operatic diva can equal. It can strike a new visitor dumb for moments. Peacock take-off is a breathless moment; a peacock coming down from on high is somehow surrounded by invisible exclamation marks.

Of course peacocks, like any other performers, need the right stage. Triple-fronted brick veneer is just not it. Gables can come near if numerous enough. Classic can make them the focal point easily, and Georgian, Victorian and some kinds of Edwardian can make it with the right garden.

You could vision peacocks in the old house I

am writing about. Of vintage late 1850s or early 1860s, but nearer to classicism than Victorianism, with mellowed, handmade bricks, with double chimneys rising above two storeys, and verandahs surrounding it on six sides, it was highly suitable for the species.

How they came around corners! How they alighted and balanced and strutted on the wooden rails which topped the ornamental ironwork at the front and sides of the house! They seem to take an extra pride — and it's not for nothing that there is a pride of peacocks as well as of lions — in showing how high they can lift their feet during dancing or, with wings drooping, how wide they can spread their gorgeous tails.

That was so in their heyday with us, in the golden summers of the peacocks when they lived at Jinwirringee.

They came to us as suddenly as they did with that instant conjuration by Daniel on the first day of our ownership. Then the day was dull and dying; now they came to us in the morning and out of the blue.

There was no preamble such as, do you want (or would you like) a gift of peacocks? They just arrived — not standing there shining out of our imaginations as they did before, but with their feet tied together with cloth and lying in the back of a blue

Mercedes Benz motorcar. 'We've brought you some birds. They'll be so very right at Jinwirringee that we brought them to show you. You do want them? Well, just keep them shut up for two weeks, while they forget where they came from, and they'll never leave you. Now where shall we put them until they're at home?' Such simple words to introduce the splendour of two young male peacocks with their tails almost fully grown.

At the east end of the stables, on tall, thick tree-trunk supports like those in the stalls, was an old tank which would once have supplied water to the resident horses. The passionfruit vines which were now making walls of green around the poles also made a good shelter from the winds. Protection from sun and rain was given by the tank itself, now grown so picturesquely beautiful with red rust as to be a positive jewel in the landscape. A wrapping of wire-netting up as far as the metal was all that was needed to make a royal residence for peacocks.

But the moment the length of the beautiful young birds was placed therein we began to realize it as a prison, because we knew they had been free from the moment they stepped from the eggs.

They would not, we were told, have been captured and taken from the width of their roaming had they followed the habits of their relatives and roosted each night with the domestic fowls. Instead it had come about that the Mercedes motorcar was now identified for a hundred kilometres around by the fact that it was covered in peacock droppings. It appears that a Mercedes can only bear so much without losing status.

Here Daniel, quite frankly besotted with the birds while they were still lying with their legs tied, was heard distinctly to say that, as far as he was concerned peacock droppings could only lend *cachet* to a Kombi Van.

But from the time a cast-iron bed-end, making an improvised gate, was closed on the birds, Daniel's mind was in there with them and feeling the evils of their incarceration. He pampered them with everything he thought they could conceive as a delicacy. At frequent intervals he left his work to excuse to them his action of confinement, and to console and compassionate their restlessness. In the dark of night he walked softly around them to see if they were suffering from fear of the fox, or perhaps had insomnia. He raved over their beauty to anyone who would stay still enough to listen.

On the eighth day of the peacocks' imprisonment two feathers were discovered to have fallen from them. They were not even very large feathers, but to Daniel they were heralds of sickness unto death. They must already have been confined for too long. 'And what if someone should happen to bring a visitor who happens to be from the RSPCA? What if somebody tells the police we are being cruel to animals? Maybe we should put them in the stables where they can run around without being seen.'

I was indignant. 'You can't confine them in stone walls where they couldn't even see the daylight properly, or where they wouldn't be able to react in any way at all to world events! That would be real cruelty! And they're not really squashed in. They can take at least ten steps each way, which is probably more than most prisoners.' And then, with what was supposed to be perspicacity, 'It seems to me that you're trying to suffer more than they are. And don't forget they've got each other as consolation.'

'Oh, I suppose so. I suppose you're right. But you know I feel for them especially because, like us who were confined during the War, there is no known end to the incarceration. For all they know, what they are suffering might be just a prelude to death. They may even have gathered from their experiences of the farmyard that prisoners are sometimes too expensive to keep.'

'Well, they might be more intelligent than we know, but I doubt if the history that's locked up in their heads is as horribly comprehensive as ours. Look, they don't seem to be at all depressed.'

Daniel had to laugh. 'Yes, they do have small heads, especially for all that grandeur. But, for all that, they look knowing enough to be even engineering a prison break! All right, my dear, I'll try to be patient.'

But, in the evening, he found a couple more dropped feathers. He wondered if the peacocks might be pulling them out on purpose — staging something of a protest. It was too much for him. He spread food on the ground outside and opened the door. The birds came out with royal poise and looked around just once. From where they were they could see neither the mountains nor the rivers, but they shivered their plumage in the free evening breeze and looked into the distance. Then, despite the endearments and supplications which were pouring from Daniel, they took long strides out into the open, lifted themselves into very smooth take-off, and were soon high in the fading blue above. We could just see them level out as they passed over the river and took the direction of the town — roughly on the way to their erstwhile home.

'Oh, dear! I think I'd better go after them!' cried Daniel, at once remorseful and anxious not to catch my eye while searching in his pockets for the keys of the van. 'My fault, my stupid fault, but probably they won't fly far in the dusk. I'll go into town and tell people to watch out for them, now and in the morning. Don't worry, I'll get them somehow. They belong to Jinwirringee even if they don't know it yet, and I promise I'll bring them back to you!'

Not that night, though, nor the next morning, although we were touring the streets by sun-up. We rang their former owners without success. We put an advertisement in the local paper advertising for two lost peacocks, and offering a reward.

Seven days later we received an early morning call.

'They were here! They were here! I go out to feed the bloody chooks and there's these bloody great birds — one sitting on the high wire fence, the other one on the ground with the chooks. I can't hardly believe my bloody eyes! Then they see me and take off. Never bloody well seen anything like it in my life. They went over the cemetery way. Wife told me about your ad in the paper. I'd come and try to help you get them, but I'm off to work right this minute.'

So we rang our builder friend, Tim, and picked him up at his house.

We didn't really expect to see anything of the birds when we got to the old cemetery. It was on the side of a gentle hill and mostly wide open to the sky. Only here and there a small tree or shrub grew amongst the graves, but a variety of tall fir tree had been planted on the lower side to divide them off from the liveliness of the town.

The birds were in the middle, picking at morsels among all that remained of the tragedy and comedy of the town's early history.

With absurd hope in our hearts we three began to move in on them. We were very near before they realized us. Perhaps because we were so close, perhaps because the gravestones loomed in front of their eyes, they didn't attempt to fly. They simply ran hither and thither among the obstructions, giving out great screeches of alarm.

We ran after them. We didn't show the same respect for the graves as they did. We were leaping onto and over marble and granite and limestone, and avoiding grave ornaments or low fences of cast-iron. Over the memorials to early settlers and late we scuttled, while I automatically took to myself the names as I passed.

Most of the graves in the Protestant part were of British origin and therefore familiar. In the Catholic section to which we were led by the birds there was more variety and more decoration. Vaulting over or skirting O'Brien, Connelly, McSporran and Milberry, Schmidt, deBurgh, Constantiano, Universitas, Tarecsinski, Mulitov and Li Po, one brushed against guardian angels, exposed Sacred Hearts, tender Saviours, mourning doves, and crosses of all sizes and splendours. I almost forgot to encircle peacocks.

It was Tim, seventy-five years old and somewhat troubled in the joints, who was successful at last. He brought his quarry down with what was considered one of the most beautiful flying tackles ever beheld, then raised himself with care to place his prize proudly in Daniel's arms.

The other bird uttered one last woeful screech, committed the sacrilege of jumping onto a tombstone, and precipitated itself from the edge of the smooth surface to ascend to the top of the tallest monkey-puzzle tree. There it sat like a glittering weathervane and surveyed the calamity of its brother being borne away by human hands.

As Daniel said, there was more space now in the tankstand pen, room for the sole peacock to move as restlessly as it wished from early morning until night. Contrary to our hopes its brother did not immediately seek it out for consolation, but rumours of its local presence were rife in the town.

Every day at least two persons would ring us to say they had seen the bird near their own or others' fowlpens in the morning, but inspecting rather than lingering. Once it was reported as having escaped the attack of a dog by blowing its feathers up to an immense size before flying off. Neighbours saw it at the river not half a kilometre away. After that nothing for a week.

When it came to its fellow at last, we did nothing for a day. Then Daniel, with unexpected country cunning, managed to trap it by tying the enclosed one to the far side of its prison and opening the door. When the two had had a couple of days together he let the first captive out. Except that it went high in the elm to roost it kept close to its mate.

A few more days and the pair were reunited in freedom.

They did not go away for a while. After the vicissitudes of their separation they were willing to treat Jinwirringee as their home — a home which they were at liberty to leave and to which they always returned. They came to us regularly for roosting and breakfast and dinner, but never ate until their servant had retreated to a distance of about three metres. Memory was strong in them. As strong as it was about keeping out of reach of the fox.

They slept at the top of the giant walnut trees, and they visited us personally, me if I was working outside, Daniel most mornings that he worked in his open workshop. Although they were two boys they often displayed or danced for us, or themselves, or for all of us.

Their favourite spot was on the railings between Daniel and the Kombi Van. They were engrossed with his movements. Who could tell what they wanted, or what they and the sculptor received from each other, except that it was joy? It was like:

In the old days
In the old days of Shey
Everyone wore brocade of dragons

And danced like peacocks

In the old days
In the old days of Shey

Everyone wore shawls of silk
And belts of pure sheepswool
And danced like peacocks.*

* Old folksong from Ladakh

— CHAPTER SIX —

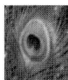

Bones

IN OUR EARLY DAYS AT Jinwirringie, Tim, the builder, was a feature of our lives. We felt he must have been born one of those rare little boys who build up their first toy blocks and leave them standing so they can be improved upon. When grown into a tall, well-built, young man he had had no difficulty in deciding to become a builder by profession. Now, in his retired years, he asserted that he had gained new life by advising and helping us without pay in the first year or two of our work on the homestead.

It was his very young grandson who, looking around at the depressing walls, asked if we were going to try to turn all this back into a house. Standing in the doorway of the wall which had been erected across one end of the dining room in order to make a kitchen in the main building, he was looking in one direction to a desecrated open fireplace plastered over with cement render and thin slabs of stone, and with a battered kerosene heater standing in front. In the opposite direction his city eyes looked

65

through a mistreated sash window which was only partially able to open or close because of the sink which had been inserted beneath, and whose lighting and viewing purposes were also impeded by the rust-streaked and sagging water tank three metres away.

'You'll be surprised', replied Tim to his young questioner. His experienced builder's X-ray vision was readily able to see through the accretions of changing fashion or stark necessity to the arched brick fireplace waiting behind the rendering; and he had already discovered the fine old cedar mantelpiece which had lain for years in one of the forgotten attics.

My own insight was at least partially able to visualize what would happen when the intrusive wall was finally broken down to make restoration complete. But in those days I hardly knew from one month to another what would be the next area of change, let alone knowing that the wall's end would come on the same day as that on which a far more famous Wall fell with far less predictable results.

Daniel and Tim and I were together on another day which had far-reaching effects on us.

We were not doing anything as spectacular as crashing through barriers, because there were many more pressing things to be done in order to live with dignity, and to reduce what Daniel regarded as a looming mass of interruptions to work which he felt could be done by no other hands than his.

The removal and replacement of the deeply-layered patchwork of old linoleum in dining, kitchen and breakfast rooms was allowed to be a necessity as long as he made the decisions and Tim oversaw the work. We three were together to make the last inspections and to assess what was needed for possible repairs to floors and high, ridged skirting boards. Suspicion of damp in the outside kitchen-breakfast room wall was aroused by a strip of tin covering the junction of the two.

Because the broad granite foundations that ran like miniature walls between room spaces made it impossible to crawl from underneath one room to another, in that house there was a manhole cut in the floor of every room we had so far needed to inspect. There was none in the kitchen because it had once been part of the dining room. Tim cut one of about seventy by seventy centimetres. As he did so he remarked once again on the thickness of the floorboards and the tenacity of the handmade nails which were still guiltless of rust.

When the square was lifted we other two were standing by the tall, spare figure of the kneeling builder, looking down, anxious that the house should retain its unblemished record of having no damp.

It was quite dry down there where the bones were.

They were very old and dry bones. They lay in the shape of most of the lower part of a slender human form, with a human forearm and a hand with long fingers neatly along each side. The upper part of the body, the ankles and the whole of both feet were concealed from sight by the edges of the square.

Daniel and myself had almost at once gone down on our knees beside the cavity, but it was some time before any of the three of us so gathered around its perimeter was able to venture as much as a word.

It was Tim, at last, in little more than a whisper, 'The floor untouched, I swear! The nails handmade! She must have been put down there more than a hundred years ago!'

'She?'

'She?'

'Yes. I'm sure it's a girl — a very young woman. There are several things which say so — the pelvic conformation, the delicacy of the femur, the long, slight bones of the hands. I learned a lot when my daughter was doing medicine. I feel this was probably a young Aboriginal woman — they have very light bones.'

Daniel spoke with difficulty. 'What are you saying, Tim? Are you trying to tell us that this girl was put here a century and a quarter ago, when the place was being built? Are you suggesting she was killed — that she was *murdered*?'

'I'm saying what I think is a likely explanation of the way she is lying so neatly, without one scrap of anything which might be clothing. At the time this house was constructed it would have been quite easy to make a young Aboriginal girl disappear without a trace. The tribes around here were in great trouble, having been already largely wiped out by disease or the forcible techniques of the whites, or just by having been effectively driven away by starvation and fear. This girl may have been a nuisance to the squatters even through no fault of her own. Perhaps she was pregnant? Who knows? Who will ever know? Or she may even have learned something which was dangerous to the family who employed her. But whoever did it has been careful to leave no traces — not a scrap of anything to give anyone the least clue.' He paused, but as we said nothing went on.

'Don't you see that she can only be a victim? Nobody ends up as she is of their own choice, or without the builders of this room having known she was here.'

'Oh, don't! Don't!' I cried, feeling the painfulness of her youth, her dilemma, her danger, her tragedy, in relentless imagination.

Tim said, 'You say "don't" because you don't want to believe it. I can picture, I can almost hear the one-day commotion it would make, with the

Missus saying to whoever would listen' — he mimicked a very English female voice — 'That Annabel (or Maggie, or whatever name they had chosen for her) has gone walkabout again! I went into the laundry and the copper wasn't even lit for the washing. But nobody had told me! None of the other lubras said as much as a word, even when I taxed them with it. You struggle and struggle to teach them a few civilized practices, and what do you get for it? They just leave and go walkabout when the feeling takes them. Dogs are more loyal! And, last Wednesday — or was it Thursday? — one of our stockmen got a spear in the leg, from ambush. I can hardly wait till we get a servant class of our own.'

Daniel said quietly, 'That's all very well, Tim, but there's not much doubt that a white man put this young girl here.'

Tim was forced to try to regain a less personal atmosphere. He took up his saw and made a gesture with it. 'Yes, well … Will we have a look at the rest of her, and maybe see how it was done?'

'No! No! No!' I tried to keep my voice calm, but it was as much wail as plea. The glances of Daniel and myself met across her bones, and I knew that his mind, as well as mine, was remembering Adam's words on the evening he had come into our bedroom. He had cried that he must go, that he could no longer go on suffering this place — acting like a white man — walking with his booted feet over what the white man did to the black. He must have felt the presence of this girl. Trembling, I said, 'No white person must look at her.'

Tim looked at me blankly, 'Here, hold on! You can't mean — you don't mean not even to tell the police?'

Daniel, greatly shaken, replied for us both. 'Yes, Tim, what Gillian says is right — not even the police — certainly not them.' His glance held mine briefly, but enough. 'Yes, she's quite right. There's no reason at all to disturb this poor girl. Even if she died by violence all those years ago nobody can be brought to justice now. And if, as you say, and we see reason in believing, she was black, I don't think any white person has a right to even know about her, much less to touch her. I'd say she has been subjected to enough handling! Let her lie there in peace since she has none to claim her. She does no harm.'

He was silent for a while, and then went on as if Tim's silence was not enough, 'Look, Tim, if we tell the police there'll be no end to it. There'll be months of investigation — or even years. There'll be endless, useless publicity, dragging on, and on, and on! Although nobody could ever be made accountable, there are descendants who would feel besmirched, there might be innocent families spoken of as being involved, and none would be able to defend either their ancestors or themselves.

'There would be innuendo, speculation and gossip every time this place was mentioned, as well as all the dredging up of old feuds; malicious and inaccurate memories would plague every warm remembrance of Jinwirringee. Resentments would grow like weeds amongst whites and Aborigines alike. And, just for that, just to inspire the worst of feelings, they would have taken these poor, childlike bones, and handled and analysed and investigated them until they were ready to put them in a glass case for people to stare at, or in a plastic bag in a numbered drawer. What good could it possibly do?

'No! No! Let us leave her here in peace — in undisturbed possession of at least this one small part of her own soil.'

Tim was convinced, and relieved enough to relax a little. 'Well, it's your say-so. It's your house. And, after all, there are none of her kin surviving. I know that because I've lived all my life here, and my father before me. If you and Gillian think you can live yours in peace knowing that she's down there, that's all right with me.'

I was getting a hold on myself. I said firmly, 'I can live with her, Tim. I know I can. I'll think of her as my secret companion. Besides, people have lived so long on this earth that there is probably no step you can take without treading on any number of them.'

'That's what I think, too, Every European certainly knows it', said Daniel, with a grateful glance, and rising to come past Tim to put his arm around my shoulders. 'That's all settled, then. We're all agreed? Eh, Tim? Look, let's nail the boards back and swear never to give her whereabouts away, nor hint of her by as much as a word — not even to discuss her amongst ourselves.' Then he had another thought. 'But first, Gillian, let's put something of our own down there with her, something to acknowledge that we knew she was there, and gave her the right to peace. If she's ever discovered, let we two be known as her friends. You, too, if you like, Tim?'

So it was settled between us, and so done. Daniel placed a small carved figure of a mother and child down there with her. I gave her one of my books, and Tim wrote, with a chisel on Huon pine wood, short words which would tell some future discoverer that we had visited this small grave in the present year and left the owner in peace.

The agreement we made was kept until there was no longer any need for silence. Now the story can be finished when the time is right to do so.

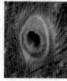

CHAPTER SEVEN

Full Flight

THE PEACOCKS WERE ONLY a small part of our own flights of inspiration at Jinwirringee, but they contributed a kind of central movement of beauty and light, symbolic of the deeper brightness of the precious living, life-giving things which were happening to us in our wonderful isolation.

*Jeden Tag mit Dir ist ein Feiertag**, we quoted to each other, revelling in having only those bonds which were of our natures or our own choosing.

It seemed that all around us, as in our own lives, northern and southern hemispheres, European and Australian atmospheres were most beautifully mingled. In this place could be seen the progression of European consciousness in a new land, with nothing left visible to draw attention to the dreadful failures and inequities which are inherent in every such development.

For Daniel, 'brought here against my will to make a little cultural manure', the house was a re-

---

* *Every day with you is a holiday.*

74

flection of his own transition, and deeply comforting. It completed at last the healing of the fracture which inevitably occurs when a person has been too suddenly divided from those visual evidences which have accompanied growth.

In deference to this duality of house as well as man, we planted northern climate trees as well as southern, but with a strong preponderance of eucalypts because Daniel now thought them the most beautiful trees in the world. Because our favorites were the wonderful river redgums, we planted the big Australians so that, except from up on the slopes of the nearby hills, no other building could interfere with the sight of Jinwirringee Homestead.

We revelled in all the dimensions around us. Height, width, depth seemed to be ever coalesced within us. Daniel's response to the spaciousness was reflected not only in the flowing lines of his work, but in the clarity of its focus. For some years past he had ceased to visually redefine anything of the old order, but sought to reveal what was inherent in the new country. His earliest ambition with his wood sculpture had been to achieve lines which truly reflected the originality of the material. In his new freedom of concentrating on wood he was now succeeding in bringing to light those hidden shapes which were both a tribute to and a continuity of the beauty innate in the whole vibrant life of trees.

But whatever Daniel made, he was always a man obsessed by the poetry of making, and no difficulty would stop him.

Though his work had the grace of apparent simplicity it was not always as effortless as it appeared — except on those rare, beautiful, and wholly to be trusted occasions of rare insight for which all artists are eternally grateful.

The aligning of the material with the idea through all the stages of creation was not always easy even for him. There were days when the clouds of uncertainty seemed to be resting just above the eyebrows, the spirit of creativity to be wilfully absent. Sometimes he would even come to me with a tragic face, sighing that nobody other than a sculptor could possibly know what a struggle it was to make visible in matter something which should show forth as emanation of spirit.

Once, in a similar unsinging condition, I replied that he could at least see the material he was shaping, and so measure the emergence of his thought. Making abstractions speak was certainly difficult, but at least it did not have to be structured out of sounds which were known to have an infinity of different and unpredictable meanings in accord with the background of the reader.

To which he replied that working with wood was more final than with written words. One could replace words with others and yet with others, but the axe, the chisel and the saw made things as separate as ever *la Guillotine*.

I shivered at the thought of having to abide with every action as I went along, yet the difficulties of creating in any media are basically the same. There is usually need for very careful focus in the time between the reception of the idea and the knowledge that something intelligent has begun to live and will thenceforward help to create itself.

For most artists, finding the point of view from which to place the idea in a true perspective so that the viewer or reader will have adequate sight of it right from the first encounter is probably the most vital problem, because the point of view must embrace continuance. If it is presented from this or that angle will it allow the creator to develop the theme so the viewer can begin to travel alongside? From here can it be developed and expanded without losing its originality? And so *ad infinitum*.

At other times the idea gets loose without going actually going out of view. It seems to wilfully evade discipline.

> *The falcon cannot hear the falconer,*
> *Things fall apart, the centre cannot hold.* *

My diaries of the Jinwirringee years bring up

W. B. Yeats, The Second Coming.

desperate scratchings in shallow earth as well as sometimes the joy of the eagle in the gyre. They are interesting to recall now that perspectives are for me both wider and deeper.

There are entries of every kind of doubt, interspersed with joy and success. These in a matter of months:

I'm reading Solzhenitsyn's 'One Day in the Life of Ivan Denisovich'. Surely one cannot be as meagre and self-centred after this experience! And the author is so technically superb that he can get the wide view even while making his lens focus beautifully on the smallest detail. But how can somebody like myself stay still enough to focus on anything?

Went to Spectrum Publications to discuss the dust jacket for 'From an Australian Homestead'. The small book is printed, bound and inevitable. I came home full of terror about the forthcoming exposure of my weakness as a poet, even though I have survived many of the poems being published in quarterlies and anthologies. If I ever come back to this earth I swear I will make poetry the foremost thing in my life. Would it be better to be a male for that? I know the pattern of female lives is obstructive, but surely a lot of it is our own choice. For instance, do I really need to restore this house further? It's liveable as it is.

Today is a day of surface-scratching nothings —

tearing at weeds as I pass, running for a bucket of water for a drooping plant, mourning over what the heat is doing to others, finding mouse-dirt on the shelf of a cupboard I am cleaning out to take books. How can one be a writer when one day can illustrate such a lack of self-discipline?

Big day today! The advance copies of 'From an Australian Homestead' have arrived! Spectrum secretary told me the book was beautiful, and it truly is. One can handle it with pleasure; the David Voigt and Sue Dent sketches come up very well, and the paper is lovely. But what about the content? There's the rub — how do I judge?

The beloved editor of my other books rang me (with tears streaming down her face, she said) to thank me. Now I feel that all is well with this one, even if no other person should tell me they like it.

Within the span of time covered by the above entries Daniel and myself (to a lesser extent) were working for one month as artists-in-residence at a nearby city festival. He had been taken around the outskirts of the city by a logging contractor, and had eventually settled for a log so large that I feared that making whatever he had in mind would take months or years instead of weeks. The contractor also brought it to the site and positioned it.

Daniel is on top of the world these days, working on his great sculpture, already named 'Out of the Deep'. It is near the edge of the car park beside the civic centre. He is talking to people singly or in groups, to crowds of school children, to the media. He is being a Very Important Person without even knowing it. If he had to do this without a woodworking tool in his hand he would never manage it. He has appeared twice on television and in several newspapers.

Today the Melbourne Sun *gave him an item in 'A Place in the Sun', finishing thus: 'The sculptor says only the wood tells him what to do. Some of those old river redgums around the city must have his ears burning!'*

Around this time, too, I began to think that the history of the homestead, as far as we could discover it, should also be written, not the least because it had been so near to becoming a building which no longer reflected its own time, place and purpose, but also because if it were done it could contain warnings of danger for coming generations.

I remember the day on which I learned of an important incident in its history and decided it *must* be done. I read of how the discoverer of gold in the Buckland Valley had stayed at the homestead on his return journey, after registering his mining claim. The date was 1853. Was it this house, or part of it?

Verified photos of the early 1870s show it in its present form, in a weathered state, with iron already over shingles, except on the small verandahs (no longer in existence) at the ends of the wings.

The history was published in 1981 and gratifyingly and continuingly well received. Perhaps the urge to make a better show of what we had already done made me begin, in late 1982, against some opposition from Daniel, to work for two hours each day to restore the front of the stables. By this time they had been repaired to a state where they would last for another hundred years, but they were not returned to the appearance which they would now have if they had been normally cared for. I convinced Daniel at last that the work was necessary by pointing out that, despite his great efforts, they still looked as though they were ready to be knocked down. A few weeks (?) of work on my part would put the seal on all he had done. Besides, he looked out from them the whole day through, while they were almost always in my perspective, and not at all pleasing.

I know that, even with some awareness of the unity of all life, we can never enter fully into the perspective of another being, no matter how much we empty ourselves to do so. This is because it is only the personal self which can fully live life from whatever point of view it has attained. Daniel could never believe that I could believe it was right for me to do anything so time-wasting as improving the facade of anything.

Many differences between Daniel and myself could be accounted for by the fact that my body and mind moved more spontaneously than his. I think he had, all in all, more clarity of vision, both because of his inner stillness and his more deliberate physical movement, both of which protected him from momentary distractions. The pieces of his work which were put aside to wait for further inspiration were never far from his memory; they remained a part of his developing life, something which his thought would in the end verify.

He would stay in his workplaces day after day, hour after hour, morning and afternoon, through till dark, without seeming to look elsewhere than at what he was making. And he was strong enough in body and mind to respond to it again in the evening if it called him. While all the while I, perhaps partly because I have such joy in movement and distrust in the self which is the vehicle of inspiration, am only contained enough to begin regularly at the task, but not intent enough to believe that this work of mine has priority over all else in my world. Nor am I able, as Daniel is, whether inside or out, to metaphorically or actually pull down a blind between myself and the wonderful, alluring world of nature.

So I suffer because of my own inadequacies and comfort myself with the hardships of other women in like situation, especially with words like those Virginia Woolf wrote in her diary:

I write two pages of arrant nonsense after straining. I write variations of every sentence: compromises, bad starts, possibilities, till my book is a lunatic's dream.

I write in my diary:

Amen to that, but for her, it was the lunatic's dream of a genius.

Despite personal peculiarities we were moving in a time when we felt we were being given the space we needed to do worthwhile things in every aspect of our living. Without the major distractions which had hitherto characterized our lives, we were often sublimated enough to feel ourselves to have left actuality and become almost diffused with the joy of knowing that ideas could take root in us and grow.

And all the while there were the people who came to us from the new life and the old, joining the two together in a vibrant continuum.

Daniel's exhibitions in other places were all successful, although we did not continue the outward movement in the way we had planned. There seemed to be too much innerness where we were. He fulfilled commissions when he felt like it, but kept himself as free as possible because freedom was the reason why we were living at Jinwirringee.

My publishers loved me. The two books of mine which had been read on ABC National Radio had film contracts and ardent supporters in what seemed to be the right places, in the Australian Film Commission as well as the ABC. The book of short stories, *A Private Viewing*, was published late in 1982. There seemed to be prospects and roads in every direction. The one I took had the homestead full in view, and it made a difference to me.

But before we were able to evaluate right roads or wrong there were lots of other joys. According to the Diary:

> *Today my three stories arrived, printed in CZECHO-SLOVAKIAN in the publication SVETOVA LITERATURA!*
>
> *They hold prominent position after a review of Australia's literary giants (among whom I am not) and have been illustrated as well as translated. I am weak with excitement, but Daniel is hyper-active with it, bent on informing the world in every possible way of what a great writer I am. It's good that only one of us has delusions of grandeur.*

Not long afterwards it was also recorded:

> *It seems that, largely because of the faith that some of the local population have in him, and the energy of*

*one in particular in pursuing it, Daniel will soon be
doing another big public work, this time on the
Ovens Highway.*

Thus alternating between frustration, despair
and delight we manage to create something. At the
end of 1985, though, I feel myself frustrated enough
to make a New Year diary Resolution:

*To keep my spirit whole; to not allow myself to
disperse myself, or to disperse others; to achieve those
goals I have set myself despite my inclination to be
always active.*

I set aside the obstreperous novel I was working on. and began another book, which was called
'Journey with a Stranger' and published in 1986.
The novel referred to would not allow itself to be
set aside for long. It eventually became a trilogy and
took years to complete.

So it was in the eighties when our creativity
was also providing money for the new golden age of
Jinwirringee under the august supervision of mountain peaks, and within sight of rivers. Within sight,
too, of farmers cultivating the land with their trac-
tors while the women came behind, planting the
plants they would later hoe, just as they would have
been doing behind the horses when the homestead
was young and the owners drove around the
countryside in carriages, instead of in big motor cars.

All appeared to be relatively the same as it had been for a very long time.

As we did those things which one or the other of us regarded as basically our duties, the homestead itself was, as in its beginning, becoming important to the people of its landscape. We were aided by many tradesmen, among whom were two of particular note — the builder, Tim, who had chased peacocks with us, and an outstanding carpenter and craftsman named Brian. To our great loss, Tim died on the way, but Brian was with us from beginning to end. With them both we had the kind of empathy which characterized the old craftsmen guilds of Europe — the kinship of those who love and honour the work of human hands.

As we and they restored the Homestead's wholeness, thought by thought, wall by wall and floor by floor, we had open days when those people of the landscape could come and be a part of it.

Sometimes they brought back to it things which had once belonged, or would seem to have belonged — things as notable as friendship, history, and stories. Sometimes they gave us important artefacts, such as horse harness, a huge old meatsafe, a butter churn, a bridal nightgown, a wonderful banqueting cloth, and many, many memories, accurate and otherwise, as memory always is, although ever subtly relevant.

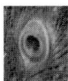

CHAPTER EIGHT

Ghosts

SOME INDIVIDUALS, LIKE myself as of now, are able to be mentally present in a familiar place, even though not visible to the eye. By contrast, it seems that others are sometimes able to present themselves to selected people in a representation of the bodies of which they were once a part, but are rarely able to communicate.

When I dwelt in a fully human way at Jinwirringee, I only contacted these spirits vaguely. By that I mean that I sensed rather than saw, or sometimes had that spiritual flash of cognition, that transcendence which is a communication beyond the usual sphere of understanding. But imagination and experience sometimes took over from the sensing to clothe the departed one in earthly form. Perhaps that was why I drifted into seeing the young creature whose bones lay under the kitchen floor as an entire person with a name. She became a girl who grew closer and more distinct as year succeeded year. Because of her I was pleased rather than apprehensive when ghosts began to materialize to a few of the many persons who visited the homestead. Daniel, too, accepted them for whatever they were. I think he would have done so even if he had seen them as solid objects — which neither of us was ever permitted, or perhaps allowed ourselves, to do. After all, what we wanted most from the spirits of Jinwirringee, was not appearance, but what they already gave us — the twin gifts of stimulation and inspiration.

The story of the first sighting reported to us at Jinwirringee is a very simple one, and happened to children unrelated to ourselves. Their parents were people of imagination and warmth, the kind of person able to see beyond the paraphernalia of personal or traditional shape and give ghosts, angels or devils individual forms which allow them to be acceptable to themselves. So it was possible that these children were more fully equipped than most to give depth to what they saw.

We offered the family the east wing where there was plenty of room in the attic. Below it, by now, were all the facilities a family could need. But the two small girls, aged seven and nine, quickly entered into the adventure possibilities of Jinwirringee and requested to sleep away from their parents, across the courtyard in the west wing with no such comforts. They had eaten their evening meal and were happily settled in the housekeepers room before we sat down to dine.

We were arrived at port when the two came into the dining room. They were welcomed and duly invited to partake of biscuits and cheese. It was only when it was suggested that they should once again retire that they requested to sleep with their parents after all.

Permission was immediate. 'Yes, of course. Of course. But you seemed to be comfortable where you were.'

'Yes. Yes, we were', they answered in chorus. 'It's just that a lady has sort of come there.'

'Really! What do you mean by a lady has sort of come?' asked one parent. The other, humouring a possible tale, added, 'But you don't think she's not a nice sort of lady?'

The answers came first from one and then the other.

'No! No! At least, we think she's all right — but she's dressed differently and she's not very — not very — well — *something* she's not.'

'You don't know what she's not?'

'No. And she just sits there.'

'She sits in the chair near the window and looks at us sometimes.'

'But she never says anything?'

'No, even when we said polite things, she just shook her head, sort of, and smiled.'

'And we can't go to sleep because she's got the light on.'

'Well, who turned it on?'

The children thought about it audibly, and decided. 'It wasn't the high-up light, so she must have brought it with her.'

It was both too simple and too complex not to be believed. Mother, careful not to be too visibly impressed, said, 'Well, go and get your things, dears, and take them upstairs.'

Father rose and followed them. There was no light visible to him in the housekeeper's room, nor could he see a visitor. Not even the cushion of the wing chair in which she had reputedly sat had retained her impression.

Following that friendly visit a young male relative of ours, attempting to sleep in the same room, was convinced then, and is to this day, that a woman whom he saw enter by the open doorway, came over to the bed and tried to strangle him.

A year later another young man of about the same age, now a successful Sydney financier, was so fiercely attacked in the same way that he spent the rest of the night on the living room couch with all the lights on. He was unnerved to the extent that he would not re-enter the room again, even accompanied and in daylight.

We never again asked a young man to sleep

there, but a lawyer girl, choosing the room despite our suggestions of other accommodation, reported on an 'eerie feeling that she was not alone', adding that reason told her there must be some subtle movement in the walls, perhaps of bird or bat, even though she had not consciously heard anything.

This sensing of another presence was, to Daniel and myself, so familiar in other parts of the house and grounds as to cause no disturbance at all. Many people who have visited historic places — especially where deeds of great injustice have taken place — have experienced the same feelings, with varying degrees of unease. We at Jinwirringee were closer than they, and more deeply involved.

The next two sightings were to people sleeping in the attic of the same wing. Both were boys and quite alone during the happening. Their separate stories each included a seated, knitting woman.

The elder said he woke in the night to see a seated female figure in the dress of the last century, busily counting knitting stitches, just as he often saw his mother do. She did not appear to be in the least interested in him, even when he essayed a greeting. After a while he fell asleep while watching her. When he awoke a couple of hours later she was still there. He couldn't go back to sleep so decided to read. Some time, he thought about an hour later, in a movement unseen by him, his visitor left him.

The other lad was far more uneasy about his spectre. He also had neither seen her come nor go. He admitted to being too frightened to seek human comfort while she was there, and even after she had disappeared was too afraid to move out in case he met her on the narrow staircase, or found her, maybe with others, waiting outside in the dark night.

None of these people had heard any of the earlier stories. All were young. Was it significant that the woman just smiled at the young girls, but was apparently knitting for the boys — the young masters whom she adored? Had her love been so dreadfully abused when they grew to be men that she thought only strangling good enough for them?

Daniel took the appearances as calling for him to sleep alone in both parts of the house, but no solitary nocturnal visitor appeared to gratify his curiosity, or tried to take his life while he slept. Our daughter, too, lived in the west attic for weeks with the same lack of either hatred or approval.

When, from time to time, we opened the homestead to the general public, it was interesting to find that the attic called forth no untoward response from any casual visitor, but the housekeepers room, now the most authentic of mid-Victorian rooms, and the homestead office, also restored, caused many sensitive people to draw back registering emotions anywhere between aversion and terror.

Perhaps the most convincing of all were the reactions of a party of female Aboriginal trainee teachers from Alice Springs Teachers College, guests of our daughter for a week some years later, and among the most enjoyable of many visitors during our time at Jinwirringee. None of them would have anything to do with the housekeepers room. They were fully at ease everywhere else — to my surprise even in the room near where we had discovered the bones under the floor boards. I wondered why the presence of the girl had been so evident to Adam and not to them. But their stay and their happiness seemed to resurrect the girl even further for me and, for a while, until my knowledge of her was as complete as it ever would be on earth, it set her moving with them, rather than apart from her race, and walking solely in my memory.

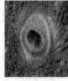

CHAPTER NINE

Mourning with Peacocks

WHEN DANIEL DIED, AND WAS not any more to be found at Jinwirringee, it no longer appealed to the peacocks. For many days they seemed to try to find the reasons for the altered state of things, the feeling of absence, the changes in sounds and silences. They no longer left to go to their usual haunts along the rivers, but walked the homestead all the daylight hours, up and down and around, searching in every place and refusing all food. As soon as I went outside, they followed me relentlessly, uttering their raucous and demanding cries even when I could hardly hear them above the noise of the ride-on mower. It was mysterious because their number-one benefactor had often been away while they lived with us, and they had not carried on in this way. Only the year before he had gone to the Centre and had been absent for three long weeks.

Those days our daughter, Kristin, and her husband, Adrian, were in the Northern Territory. Daniel's last visit had been a time of deep growth for him. He and the Aboriginal people had no trouble in relating. This time he was given opportunities to be alone with them and to work companionably alongside them in the gardens they were establishing not very far from Tennant Creek. After he returned it became evident that being in close contact with their understanding of the rhythms of the earth had given much more than personal satisfaction. He had taken the meaning of the landscape even more deeply into his heart and so, ultimately, into his work.

This year when winter had begun at Jinwirringee and the long line of orange trees was glorying in the ripening of its fruit, Daniel had, perforce, to change his mind about going north again, this time with me. He was working for a solo exhibition which had been fixed for a date earlier than expected. Ideas were welling up in his mind and he dared not leave them unfed lest they starve.

Once more I went alone into that great central amphitheatre. On its broad stage the affairs of humanity were showing forth foreign and fatal disharmonies which, because of the size of the background against which they moved, were still considered tolerable and able to be absorbed if not by earth, then by distance.

Nor could I easily believe in destruction when I was once in the wideness and the silence. I was more than happy to be received with love by my own, and to have my ego stroked into pleasure by meeting again with those who would call me by my Aboriginal name — even though the name had been bestowed for no virtue but that of connection with those considered worthy. Neither did I find myself any closer to having forgotten the Aborigine who had lived for weeks in our house. Perhaps because Adam had told us he was on an eternal quest for his mother, there was a part of me which was always on the lookout for him, and if not actually seeking him, then seeking in others for his kind of consciousness. If I could not find him in his own flesh, then I might yet discover him in a new understanding of those whom he had chosen as his people over and above his white ancestors. Even though I beheld nobody who resembled him out there, I think I moved closer to realizing why a 'lost' man would want to retain his earliest relationship.

It became even more apparent during the fort-night when Kristin and I camped out on the tray of the ute in the open country, with only a mosquito net between our eyes and the sky. The stars had all moved, the Southern Cross was much further to the south, the universe had never been so wide and strange, nor so deeply intimate.

Back at Tennant Creek I went out hunting with five Aboriginal women friends, and was amazed how at home, how *complete* I felt all the time the hunt was on, and even when the goanna was captured and killed. I had expected to be sickened by the killing, but was not. The animal was baked very lightly amongst the coals. I ate part of the tail, and was given my first witchetty grub. The food was precious, too, being one with my first taste of an elemental community experience.

I would have stayed longer in the Centre, had not a phone-call from Daniel revealed his wish for me to return, although it was cloaked in less pressing words. What he said was that from now on he was never going to let me go so far away without him. He said he had become afraid that I might discover something so wonderful that I would never return. He knew how the silence of the Interior could take hold of people and keep them forever. Then, as if he felt he had been ungenerous he added, 'But don't hurry too much, *liebling*. Stay just as long as it takes to gather up something for another book. Yes, I know I'm talking nonsense, but when you're not here there is nobody to talk rubbish but myself. Yes, yes, of course I'm working — I have more than you know to make up for. Yes, I'm very well, and there is still plenty of food in the refrigerator because people know I'm deprived, and keep bringing meals for the poor prisoner.

'Oh, dear Gillian, it's almost more than can be

borne to hear you so close, and to know that all the things I want to tell you simply can't be spoken over anything as long and loose as a telephone wire. But just wait till you get back! I think it will take a whole day and night to cover it all, to tell you the things that have happened while you've been feasting by campfires and eating roasted goannas.'

It was all authentically Daniel in his right mind, but there was something undetectable, some wistfulness which made me remember, with deepened clarity, a recent period of time when there had been something subtly amiss with him. He had shown no certain symptoms of illness, but sometimes he had been, for days and even weeks, not in his usual deeply satisfactory communion with the world — in fact often seemed to be only vaguely living in it. The light from him was not so constant.

Lately, as he began working for the exhibition, the light had returned, but the cautionary memory now returned to me with force.

With it I recalled the great Melbourne photographer, Athol Shmith, prowling ecstatically about the grounds and around the workshops of our former home, photographing away while he murmured over and over again — 'Luminosity! Luminosity! Such luminosity!'

So now I returned as soon as I could. Leaving the plane and driving the car over the last three hundred kilometres, I was almost feverish to arrive to see that Daniel was all right.

No doubt my earlier-than-expected arrival had something to do with it, but I found him in the greatest contrast to whatever it was I had expected. Always of an easily exuberant temperament, now he was so filled with life as to be effervescent with it. Its abundance overflowed into everything around him. He, who had often denied the great power of words by saying that they were full of pitfalls, no matter how wary the user, now became able to pour out the most appropriate of them with all the spontaneity of a Bach fugue.

This sure showing-forth also seemed to be present in everything in the vicinity of him. That day when I arrived it was just beginning to be evening. The winter sun sinking behind our hills was reflecting pure gold into the air above the high mountains opposite.

The peacocks perched on the rail between the open workshop and the garage were limned by its illumination. They watched with cockheaded interest while Daniel and I hugged each other and made the joyful sounds and motions belonging to the enfolding-unfolding of coming home in all senses of the word.

Then, as if to fully partake, those two male creatures jumped down from the rail and called and strutted with appropriate showing off and spreading of tails.

The sculptures being finished for the exhibition which was to come off early in the next month also absorbed the shining of the evening, showing themselves to be full of timeless meaning.

All things belonged to the air, the hills, the light. All things were one, and at the same time themselves, as they had sometimes been in the great open spaces of the Centre.

Out of the Centre and its people came at least the beginning of the story which Daniel began to relate to me.

He had awakened one morning in his room, which looked up to the stables, and seen through the window the form of a man moving in the mist which seemed to cover everything in the outside world. He couldn't make out who it was because of the thickness of the fog, which was dense enough to be displaced by movement and showed only dimly the facades of buildings. The shadowy bulk moved along them to the open workshop and disappeared into it. Then it reappeared around the other end of the stables, telling Daniel that it was a person familiar with the way through that part where he often worked when the weather was cold. Yet he knew that the appearance, even allowing for the distortion of the mist, was not that of anybody who commonly called here, or came from time to time to assist.

Still watching, he swung himself out of bed to collect his warm dressing gown and go to see who it was.

Then the man, perhaps feeling he was too early in such cold weather, came down the slope in order to pass away through the gate. In doing so he became more visible. With a joyful shout of recognition, Daniel threw open the window. 'Adam! Adam! Oh, dear God, Adam, don't go! I'm here! I'm coming.'

'It was great! Do you remember how he came that first day, all bleary-eyed, with dew in his hair and twigs sticking to his creased clothes? Now, although the fog was dampening him in the same way, he had a quite different air about him. He was alert and alive! In a couple of minutes I had him in the house and had stirred up the kitchen fire.

'Just as in the old time, he readily admitted to not having breakfasted. Whatever else was altered his appetite was just as great as ever. We had such a breakfast! I ate for a long time, too, because there was so much to tell and to listen to that we needed food and drink to sustain ourselves.'

Watching how Daniel's face shone as he recollected the scene, I thought it was well that I had not been there. As a third presence I would only have inhibited all the good talking of the failures and successes of the almost ten years since Adam had gone away from us. I imagined how he had hesitated before coming back. Perhaps, too, he had come on a day of fog in order that he might slip away again if my car was in the garage. It was only too likely that he would never again wish to see that 'real Aussie' who had betrayed him to the police.

Across my private thoughts Daniel was saying that for Adam it was as if his departure from Jinwirringee had been the beginning of the end of the road he was then journeying on. Not that it happened all at once. Life had become more and more unmanageable and unbearable in the three following years. He had been warned to stay away from area after area.

Daniel could only guess through what long agony he had at last awakened to the realization that he was gone beyond all hope of recovery by his own efforts. He told how, one desperate day, he had staggered into the casualty department of a Northern Territory Hospital and begged to be treated for the disease of alcoholism.

On another unforgettable day, when his body was raging at what it still thought of as deprivation, his wife walked into the room and sat down beside him. For a while after bringing out the last sentence Adam had become silent with emotion. When he could speak again he went on to say. 'You have to meet her some time, Daniel. She is the same race-mixture as myself, but how beautiful you will never know until you see her. She didn't make one word of reproach. She said the family wanted me very much, and I would have to drive her away if I ever wanted to be rid of her again.'

It was more than six years since that new life was first given, and she was still faithfully there. In the midst of it all another son had been born to them.

Two years ago, when the elder boy had applied to begin a university law degree, Adam had had to face a big change in his own outlook. He told Daniel what had ensued when the news of his son having gained a place had arrived.

He had faced the boy with very conflicting feelings — pride in his son fighting with fear that he would lose him entirely to the white man's way.

The boy, who had begun to know his father, seemed to understand. 'Dad, why don't you come in on it, too? You could do it standing on your head!'

'It would stand on their heads all my ideas of resisting the evils of the white man's thinking', he had heard his own voice snarling in a way to which it was no longer accustomed.

But in reply his son's tones, not even anxious, accustomed to debating in secondary school, 'If you're going to resist any thing, you have to make yourself stronger than that thing, don't you?' And while his father was digesting, 'And, Dad, if you don't like white man's way, why do you always carry in your pocket that little book called, *From the Greek*?* You must love that! Why do you read such a lot of white man's language stuff, and why do you make poetry in it sometimes? You must really love what they say.'

And Adam heard his own voice again, not so sure now. 'Well, I'd soon get sick of reading a message stick, wouldn't I? And there are so few who could read what I wrote if it were in a tribal language. You know, I have never met one person who spoke just like my mother did. There have been words the same, or almost the same, in other tribes, but not very many.'

'Maybe you could find what you want to know if you did a course at the university. And you could learn to teach all of us Aborigines how to be equal. I bet you'd get in easily, talking like you do, real white man's way. There are a lot of adult places going these days.'

Daniel was jubilant in recollecting the conversation. 'So Adam began university at the same time as his son. He's doing Arts-Law for a start, he says, but he's got his eye on Aboriginal languages.

*Various translators, T. E. Higham & C. M. Bowra (eds), Oxford University Press, 1943.

'He said it was hard to face up to in the beginning — like a tribal initiation — but, like all initiates, he was soon able to comfort himself that that period wouldn't last forever. Now, I should think he's well on the way. He's had good passes in all his assignments, and is beginning to believe in his own intrinsic value.

'The most striking change in him is that he no longer sees himself, or his family, as victims of two cultures, but as specifically and ideally important assistants in humankind's growth towards universality. Remember how he was always capable of discerning the larger issues? It was only himself he could not make out.'

Six months ago Adam had been able to announce to his family that he had also gained a position in Social Welfare. And now, with something of the same joy still in him, he brought that success with him to the homestead.

'Who better for the job? Who better?' Daniel had shouted at him. 'Who better than you who have come so triumphantly through so much suffering? Adam, you can go anywhere, do anything. You could be a professor some day, or even the chancellor of a university!'

I could visualize the expression of Daniel's own abundant joy — the hugging, the patting on the back, the shaking of hands again and again, the laughter, the feeling of not being able to adequately express his unlimited delight that Adam had come back to Jinwirringee with his happiness upon him.

To me Daniel added, 'And to think this was mostly brought about by your giving him your little book! Yes, well, don't protest too much. It must have contributed. And you can now stop complaining that you can't find another like it! It was all so right, after all, wasn't it? You can even stop blaming yourself for having called the police.'

By this time the evening was becoming colder. We moved in to Daniel's workshop amid the sculptures and the sawdust and the chisel curls while he went on with his story.

'Because Adam was now a university student, and because we were not now master and worker, he felt he could put himself into words in whatever situation we were in. He and I together had three of those wonderful days that seem to have come straight out of eternity. Often I wished you were here to share them, but there was very little of our travels in the bush and hills which could have taken place with a woman.' He became silent, once more almost overcome by recall.

'The first day we went out with the trailer and picked up a redbox tree-trunk I'd seen the last time I was there. That night we talked late. Oh, how we talked! And then I wanted him to sleep in one of the main rooms, but he insisted on staying in the East Wing, just like he did before.

'Of course when he got there he saw it wasn't possible to even accurately visualize his former residence, so he slept above in the attic. In the morning he told me he had been very happy to feel that while the restoration of Jinwirringee was taking place the same thing had been happening in him.

'On the second day of the three we did some work together for old times' sake before we went again to the hills. This time his confidence in himself allowed him to take me even further into Aboriginal relationships with the earth. I can't tell you how vividly he brought to life the people who once lived here. For me the hills are not now, and never will be, unpopulated by human beings. They walk up there the way history walks in all places.

'This time Adam told me many things about the lives and rights of the women. He went as deeply as he could into it, especially so I could pass their stories on to you. He said he knew it would make you feel good to understand.

'On the third day we were so — so *integrated* — not only with each other, but with the whole universe — well, it was just being absolutely free! I think you know what I mean.' He was silent for a full minute, remembering, before he continued with his narrative. 'That was what led us to make the ceremony — a real Aboriginal ceremony, so that we could — so that we would — I mean we took the opportunity to bury for ever the ill-feeling between black and white which, as we both know, had managed to survive almost a century and a half of changing faces here at the homestead.' For the second time that evening he was a little overcome and had to search for words. Then he added, rather hesitantly deciding,

'I'd like to tell you all of it now — but I feel I can't do it justice without you coming with me to the place of the ceremony. The thing is so big, so important, so complete, that I can't just say a few words about it. It needs the mountains to help me to put it in your mind as I received it. Can you wait? Will you be patient until I catch up a bit with the work I should have had finished days ago?'

He turned from me and looked at the extent of what must be done, and I saw it immediately displace everything else from his conscious mind. Once again I thought of an old quote which I had often consoled him with when we seemed to have not enough money. It says that those who love the labour of their hands more than the measure of success or fame have been called by the gods.

Despite the fact that my travel bag was still at my feet, the call of work was now allowed full rein.

'Now, come and give me another kiss because I can't stand here forever! I must get busy. You, too, if you're not too tired. You don't look tired, you look wonderful! You don't need to get changed to do what I want. Just walk around and use your inspiration to help me find names for the thoughts that went into each work. I've promised the catalogue details to be ready when Mrs Smith comes on Wednesday, and you know I can't do any of it without you.'

Perhaps it was happiness in finding him so well and so brightly and entirely dedicated; perhaps it was just the extent of personal involvement needed to make possible the welding together of an exhibition into a coherent whole, but I don't remember being impatient to hear his revelations of how the ghosts of Jinwirringee were laid to rest. All I could recall, when life for me returned to being something like normal, was that I had had a tinge of regret in case my little black friend whom I had recreated so lovingly from the bones under the floorboards might not be so visible to me in future.

Maybe there had been more discussion than my memory has brought me through the great blurring of the days that followed, but chiefly what I know now is that those very few weeks were ethereal with light — yes, full of labour and love and light — a most especial luminosity!

In those weeks Daniel put into words, all at one time, the things he found most beautiful in life. They came from him like a song:

'You, because you are as vibrant to me as when I first met you, and bound even closer to my heart.

'Music, because it must be the language of heaven. In the tones of music there is no misunderstanding.

'A mother and her child, because this embodies the whole of life.

'Trees, because they are the greatest helpers of all living things. Without them can nothing live or breathe. They are the greatest land and air purifiers, the greatest water engineers, the greatest shelter; they give everything of themselves. And when they die and come into my hands I can bring them back to an even more lasting beauty and life.'

I awoke one morning about three weeks after I had come home, still filled with the light, and eager for the day's work. In that ambient July we were experiencing those halcyon days which, when they come in the midst of winter, seem to be the perfection of weather — cloudless skies, air cold and fragrant, winter birds from the hills everywhere — ibis, herons, choughs, currawongs both black and grey, parrots and crows, and even two small rainbow birds

110

making a nest in the ploughed land — the rivers and the mountains singing in silent harmony.

Beside me I saw that Daniel was still sleeping. I left him undisturbed and went into the shower.

I was towelling myself when he came in. 'Good morning! Good morning! Beautiful day again! I meant to be up earlier, but never mind, there's always tomorrow. I'll make the tea, and we'll have it outside. There's a patch of sun on the front verandah just made for us. Oh, but what a morning! No, don't let's work! Just let's leave everything, and go up together to that place in the hills where I can tell my story. We'll have a whole day, a whole, whole day.' I heard his strong voice singing Beethoven's *Song of Joy* as I completed my dressing. I was about to go out to him when he came back to me clutching desperately at his body. 'I don't know — something is wrong — I can't get my breath — I want to be sick.'

How can I tell you of his great distress as I assisted him to his bed? 'Stay quietly while I call the doctor. It won't take more than a moment. Show me where the pain is worst.'

'No pain, no pain at all. I just can't get my breath! It's terrible — terrible, my darling! Don't go away from me! Don't go yet, *liebchen*.' Yet he did not appear to have trouble in talking; he was not gasping for breath. So I put my arms around him as

111

best I could, told him not to be alarmed, told him it was probably asthma, that it would not take a minute to ring for the doctor, who would bring something to help him.

The call took only seconds, but when I came back I could see a terrifying change. Life was draining from him; he was fast losing colour. He knew me and wanted to speak, but I saw he was losing consciousness while trying desperately to keep me in his vision.

Not unless such an emergency has happened personally can anybody imagine the desperation of the next few minutes. I thought he had lost breath, that there was no pulse, and so I gave him artificial respiration, blaming myself that I had not actually practised the art.

Whether or not he had really stopped breathing I will never be sure. He was breathing when help arrived, but the pulse was low and intermittent. When the doctor undid the waistband of his trousers so he would be more comfortable I remember feeling ashamed because I had not thought to do it. I remember how deliberate, how very slow, seemed the movements of the doctor, and of the ambulance men when they arrived a couple of minutes later.

The stretcher was being carried out of the wide passage doorway when I saw Daniel had stopped breathing. I remember my panic, how I begged them to put the stretcher down and do something.

The doctor put out a hand and drew me aside. 'Don't hold them up. They've got the equipment in the ambulance.'

Then, turning a little away from me, he added, 'But I don't think he is going to come out of it.'

And I realized I had known right from the moment I laid him on the bed.

The uniformed men just went on without seeming haste, carrying him through the sunlit morning over to the waiting vehicle. Then, in the emotional blank which had fallen upon me, I noted that although the stretcher seemed to be moving slowly, the legs of the men were passing each other very rapidly.

In the ambulance they tried to revive him. They went on trying at the hospital till I told them it was too late, and more than enough.

After those golden winter days together the very atmosphere of earth seemed to go into mourning. Its tears came down in torrents of rain which, despite the new insulation which had been laid between the thick, old yellow-box shingles and the ceilings, roared desperately above us on the corrugated iron roofs of Jinwirringee.

The rains moved much soil downward on the slopes, flooded the plains and the rivers, half-drowned the camping grounds, and crept into low-lying homes. They continued for the three days of waiting, damaging bridges and power and telephone installations. They made a stream across our drive so that the cars of mourners must ford it in tentative slow motion with a tractor standing by.

Despite the intensity of it, many of the crowd who had come from far and wide for the church ceremony went out to the graveside and stood there in the downpour, weeping, either externally or internally, under the weeping sky, and able only to half-hear the words of the burial service.

Turning at last from the small streams of water running down into the grave, I saw, away at the back of the crowd, an Aboriginal man. It was Adam, hatless and coatless, his face knotted with grief. He did not come forward, and nobody mentioned to me that such a man had been there. I don't think he was just a vision.

One day, I don't know how much later, I was sitting on a log under the giant elms, surrounded by un-touched seasoned wood and works just begun, and wondering how long life would go on without the transcendence of Daniel.

The peacocks came up to me there, uttering their plaintive cries. Once again I told them he was not coming back, this time adding that he was in the cemetery where we had first caught one of them, and then watched with dazzled eyes while the other flew to the very top of the monkey-puzzle tree.

They walked once around the heap of wood as though to make sure I was right, before consulting together very briefly. Then, without so much as a glance at me, they began the stretched-out run which was the beginning of their take-off. I watched them attain maximum height as they crossed the rivers, going in the direction of the town just as they had done on the day when we had ended their first imprisonment. They were never seen again by any local person. This time there was nobody to bring them back.

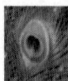

CHAPTER TEN

Interval

IN THE DAYS BETWEEN
Daniel's death and the departure of the peacocks
there were many who asked the usual questions and
offered the same solutions to problems which always arise in countries where the extended family
home is not the norm. However they were phrased
most of them said the same thing: What was I going to do with myself now I was alone? Was I going
to try to live solitary in this large house in the middle of this too-large space, so far away from family?
Surely somewhere smaller, somewhere closer? And
then they would look around with uncommitted
eyes at the numbers of the sculptures and the mass
of materials and tools which pertained to them. They
thought about the extent of the house, now even
more returned to history with simple, early Australian furniture, and wondered if I was very much attached to it. Whichever way one looked at it, moving
or not moving, how could one person deal with it
all? Perhaps they thought of being asked to fill their
sheds with it during my change of habitat. What-

ever the reason, it seemed they were mostly relieved of some obscure responsibility by what they had said.

None of the locals and few of my close friends suggested I should leave — perhaps because they had a deeper feeling for space and place. I think they understood that Jinwirringee was the only place filled with what I now needed, that it was situated in a landscape I had spent a large part of my life moving towards.

I do remember telling myself that I would stay here, like Miss Hare of Patrick White's novel *Riders in the Chariot*. Here I would live out my life alone, even though the buildings fall down, the weeds and trees move to choke me, and I become no longer strong enough to even break through cobwebs.

I ignored the fact that the time in which Jinwirringee would be allowed to crumble and be buried like White's Xanadu was at the same time just past and also very distant. And I already knew I would not be allowed to be hidden in foliage to await the Chariot of Death. I knew that my body was called upon to be more terribly and starkly visible because Daniel was not there. I would be on view from the perimeters to the centre, when those who cared came to help. You, I said to myself, you, this ageing woman already beginning to lose colour, will also be at the mercy of those people with kind faces and pitying eyes, beginning to invade. You will try to reflect the kindness, and to deflect the pity, but the you of you will not be strong enough without Daniel. Are you willing to take the risk of becoming lost?

The immediate answers were within my own life and that of Daniel. Daniel was physically gone, but his aims and my own remained. I told myself that with them I could live by myself in the homestead which had become a place through which Daniel and I could pass on our understandings of life. I thought I could allow his spirit to be always present like those others who lingered there, and perhaps, like some of them, he would be enabled to move closer with time.

I think this may have been when the ambivalence which had characterized my relationship to Jinwirringee began to have a different meaning. Up to this point there had always been Daniel to hold the balance between our selves and the house by not allowing it to count to the point of obsession. After he died I was often more in the obsessed state than the balanced.

Jinwirringee, the place visually possessed, was already, for me, spirit-held. Between it and that other more ethereal place of personal transcendence, my writing life, there had always been a distinct difference. Now, although I went to my desk as regularly as possible at the time marked off, it was most difficult to dissociate myself. Thus it was that much of the work I did then had to be reworked and rewritten.

One part of me was consciously aware of danger, but the other part was glad to have so much immediate responsibility to fill the daylight hours that my brain could not long ponder those mostly hypothetical changes in myself. So much strenuous activity was also necessary if one was to push suffering of mind down to an acceptable level and hopefully exhaust body to an extent that sleep would inevitably shorten the dreariness of evening. When I awoke each morning I was as sure of my schedule as a prisoner in jail, or a seminarian in a monastery — hours for this and hours for that until the sun should set again.

I had several areas of work in which to perform. I must keep Daniel's work alive by becoming its custodian and curator of exhibitions. I must finish the restoration of the homestead, and I must show my faith in Daniel's faith in me by completing the big writing work which I had already begun. They were all charges so sacred that I did not for one moment think of avoiding them, but I thought they must perforce be done doggedly, without pleasure in doing, or joy in accomplishment.

Day after day I worked as though I was to be judged on how much I could press into the daylight hours. In that pushed-down part of my mind I think I was believing that this frenzied activity would lead to a shortening of the time of inhabiting the earth without Daniel.

As time went on, though, I noticed that some of the things he had loved me to do, like the writing of a regular diary, were allowed to become spasmodic. The reason could be that there was nobody to please, or, on the other hand, nothing seemed so vividly personal as to be worth recording. I was rapidly becoming a hostage to the needs of the things around me — perhaps one which the homestead had accepted until reimbursed for the indignities which had been put upon it. I was certainly not able to envisage what that repayment would be. Everything must be subsumed to the visible tasks. Some of those tasks depended on immediate resolution on what to do first.

There was more money needed for restoration than there had been when Daniel was around to take part. Times of ready cash had occurred spasmodically in our lives. We were by profession either in debt or flourishing. This was why we had already been some ten years on the job of restoration. Now, without Daniel to be insouciant about it, I must approach the problem in as business-like a manner as my nature would allow. Made realistic because of his death, I felt that everything which needed to be done should be done as nearly as possible at once, because death for me, as for Daniel, might not come with a forewarning, but as the great beast springing and dividing,

So, when I was at last alone, I looked around me and made my first list of priorities. Like most things which have presented themselves as ideas, the tasks attained more reality when able to stare back from a sheet of paper scrawled with symbols of language. They instantly demanded reasoning, a time frame, a priority.

I became aware that reasoning was very different now that it was being applied without having to find acceptance by another.

Daniel never made a move to do any work but his own, for any other was an intrusion into his precious time — how precious I did not then fully know.

Work, for Daniel, was the fine balance-wheel of existence. In its order all inspiration was realized and shown forth. Through its agency he became one with creation and was able to communicate with his fellows as if all people had the same perception. It was through his work that he found peace of mind, stability in adversity, and renewal of spirit.

Once, when he was engaged in public on a very large sculpture, a great scientist who had been brought to view it was asked by a TV reporter what he thought of the work. He replied, 'It is the best that man can do, the highest he may reach.'

Such scientists, of the best in the world, whose work related to the life of the universe, were often brought to Jinwirringee. Always, so said their letters, both before and after Daniel's death, they were left with some kind of new dimension in their lives. It was mostly through them that eleven of those 'high works' were to reach Europe and America in the first year after Daniel died.

In the meantime I saw that it was important to have him continue to speak in the way he most preferred, by letting the planned exhibition, already catalogued, go ahead.

Although there were many sculptures, in a variety of media, standing about the place, this show was to be entirely of wood. I was glad, because the wood alone seemed to show the entire spirit of the man.

It was a time of great torment for me, but successful in every way. All that was left of what had been shown were the very large works.

There were still plenty of pieces, large and small, either decorating the place, or in the workshops. Most of them were those for which either Daniel or I had particular love. Daniel, of course, rarely wanted to sell anything; he just wanted them to be showing what he thought. Therefore I intended that there would be a permanent place for them to do just that.

We had already restored the whole of the stables to a state where they were safe to stand for a long, long time, and had used them for years to store and sometimes show as much sculpture as could be got up the stairs and through the loft door. Larger pieces were mostly in the back of the attached open workshop, one of the places where the peacocks strutted while Daniel worked.

Apart from a need for roof repairs and strengthening, the main thing lacking in the long loft was natural light. It had no windows except for one at the far end from the doorway. As this had been filled for years with a chunky, coloured-glass and crystal creation of Daniel's, the light was, however beautifully, too interrupted and too solitary to be useful to other works. We needed to claim some of the south-eastern illumination now being so passively reflected from the outside of the high brick wall.

It was decided to let it in through suitable windows to be set between the massive buttresses which Daniel had built in support of the whole building. The project would in no way interfere with the original unity of the northeast-facing stables.

After the darkness of the latter half of that winter, the spring was late, but I remember how suddenly I realized its undeniable growth was budding its way up through pain with all the authority and appeal of a hallucinating drug.

The mountains came clearer and clearer, nearer and nearer, the snow took on the shapes of melting. Once, driving towards the east from the main town, I saw a whole other town, with high buildings and steeples of ice, where no town could actually have been.

Water birds came back to the dams, magpies claimed sole occupation of trees and all the empire which could be seen from the nest, thrushes sang in the walnut trees at noon, just as though Daniel had not died. Swallows built and began sitting underneath the eaves, small bright birds darted after insects, ducks led their golden hatchlings across the waterholes, and there were many calves in the paddocks.

The year was once more filled with resonating life. The increasing light of it revealed to me that if I took such a positive step towards it as opening the dark wall of the stable would involve, I would simultaneously be admitting its fullness as once more a force in my life.

Seeing that I had such a responsibility to Daniel's memory I had no choice but to agree. So, under the hands of the ever-resourceful Brian, ideas became visibilities, and the studio grew into what it should be for showing sculptures.

Not only was the coming in of the light a confirmation of spring accepted, but a creative satisfaction. It brought with it a desire to do more. Visions of possibilities so spread themselves out before me that I was induced to make plans which would enable the loft of the stables to be used for human habitation — perhaps a place for me to hide and write when my dedicated tasks were finished or the care of house and grounds became too much for me. That idea must have made me smile ironically at the time, but the sketch continued to flow from my fingers as though propelled by a force beyond myself. This special life had not been in me for many months. Temporarily it filled my being as with fire, and left me clean and luminous.

It did not surprise me that this inwardly inspired plan was accepted without alteration by the local authorities, the Historic Buildings Council and the National Trust — by the last two because it was felt it could make a contribution to the longevity of the place.

For me it remained more than that. Transcendence had not completely passed away with Daniel, after all. There was a renewed ache towards his single sort of dedication, which would not have allowed him, even in like circumstances to mine, to voluntarily give time to anything less.

Yet I was a woman still divided, dedicated and fearful — one who, if work did not go forward steadily, could soon be essentially lost in despair and grief. Maybe this was partly why I gave renewed assent to something promised before Daniel died. It was the holding of a Garden Party Fete at Jinwirringee for the Red Cross.

It was a Big Event, embracing costumes, customs and occupations from the nineteenth century, and several branches of the Red Cross as well as the general public took part. To the sound of an excellent bush band it went off splendidly, while the giant Red Cross flag of service to humanity flew overhead.

I didn't know then that if you once willingly let the spirit of music have free rein in a place it will take over; but that seems to be when the dream that Daniel and I had dreamed together, of bringing back the basic harmonies of Jinwirringee to such an extent that music would begin to grow naturally in it, began to take reality and be heard again by human ears. We had proved the possibilities to ourselves years before when two first-class artists from England had led us in the singing of Christmas carols, but now we were experiencing the reality.

From the time when Kristin, Adrian and Sally came down from the Centre and began sharing the life of the homestead, it became even more a place for making music. There was music of all kinds willing to be made there — music beneath the trees, music on the verandahs, in the courtyard, in the loft of the stables, all flowing above the music that was the homestead's natural environment. For good measure, though not yet so abundantly, there was poetry, and dancing on the grass.

As a background to all this, the work of enhancing and maintaining the buildings and the acres of garden and lawn still went on at some sort of fever pitch. Some times I was so deeply immersed as to scarcely know whether I was grieving or not.

On one of those days, not long after the Red Cross event, I was surprised when I caught sight, in the glass window of a shop, of a haggard stranger walking parallel to myself. In a way that was what I was — a being hardly inside myself and strangely parallelled by a worker who walked beside me.

Perhaps this otherness was what made a woman stop me in the street to say, 'You don't know who I am, but there are many like me. We all know who you are. We know all about Daniel and yourself. We want you to know we love you both; we love your work, and we always will.'

It was through all these happenings as well as everything around me that I was at home at Jinwirringee. This at-one-ness, which I had so shared with Daniel, may have been partly because of the situation of the homestead. We had each been born on the side of a hill overlooking a river valley, but it was only at Jinwirringee that we realized that all the homes we had selected to live in had had, although different, the same basic characteristics. Perhaps all

127

those who have remembered their childhood happinesses in a certain place seek to re-establish the beloved landscape before moving back to the safety of the good earth.

In the meantime I loved all around me, and most of all the appearances and implications of Daniel's work — which I never for a moment regarded as anything less than his life added to the lives of trees and now existing as a living force.

Like many a greater poet-writer, I have seen, from time to time, glimpses of the universal and communal reality of all things. In 1979, when Adam was with us, I'd written a poem which included the lines:

> *Earth's moving cataracts of history*
> *all broaden to a common beam*
> *an active dream*
> *where no part of the long progress*
> *stands alone*
> *where human hands*
> *touch at the same time*
> *acropolis and lunar probe*
> *computer key and fossil bone*
> *book and axe of stone.*

My reactions to the sculptures did not always feel universal. Sometimes they were intensely, almost unbearably personal. Sometimes I would go and lean

128

against the Phoenix Tree on the Ovens Highway, and seek to experience Daniel again. This great tree, torn up by its roots to become a symbol, had been, like himself, removed far from a beloved early life to become, as he had said, 'in this place, just a little cultural manure'.

One illustration of this fertilization having brought positive results happened when I was called to attend a ceremony at the National Trust ship, *Polly Woodside*, where a bronze plaque in memory of Daniel and his volunteer work was to be unveiled. Most prominent is the ship's figurehead carved by him in Huon pine.

It was a moving ceremony in honour of one who had arrived here under conditions as inauspicious as those of the early convicts. When the flag was lowered to half-mast, and the notes of the Last Post floated on the evening air, I thought of how, for seven long years, Daniel had listened to that lonely tune marking off, for the soldiers of the prisoner-of-war camp, and every one of its inmates, another of the days that seemed to stretch into an interminable future. The future, however, had brought him to happiness and fulfilment. Now his life seemed to be appropriately rounded by this paradoxical tribute from the country he had chosen as his new homeland, and had come to love above all others.

— CHAPTER ELEVEN—

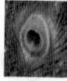

The Coming of Light

DANIEL HAD BEEN GONE from my sight for a little less than two years before it came to be the right time to undertake the last restoration ceremony. It would have been very difficult for him to accede to it.

To reduce the work of others to a pile of rubbish when that work was still in good order and doing what it was meant to do, would have been abhorrent to him. His first argument would probably have been that, considering the amount of uncluttered space around us, the resentment of a minor division, which could not be said to interfere with our way of life, must be an act of discontent rather than of restoration.

Through all the long haul of giving back to the homestead its original beauty he was apt to weigh up the advantages of accepting the status quo as much as possible in order to conserve our precious time. To accept life as it happened to be was a part of his philosophy as long as he had his work, and his own people were acting harmoniously. It would have been a hard task to convince him that the coming disharmony would be worthwhile. Or to lead him to understand what I did not then fully understand myself — that what I was doing for the house was as much a part of my own creativity as the more obvious one of writing.

Argument may not have succeeded, and I would have had to take the second step of getting him to believe that his consent was vital to my ease of mind and thus to my future as a writer. Even after this idea had begun to grow within him, there would have been a need to make him believe that having workmen on the place would not necessarily invade his privacy and take weeks of creativity away from his life.

In the matter of his own private place Daniel was as territorial as any magpie. No unauthorized person could cross the boundary of any of his workshops, none uninvited could even walk amongst the curing timber sprawled on the ground behind the stables. One young woman who quite rightly thought the potential from which Daniel worked was part of his genius, took some of her visitors through it. Her action brought down upon her such almost-silent but still effectively-expressed wrath that she went in fear and trembling of the normally mild Daniel for the rest of his life. Only after he died did she dare even to ask to own some of his work.

There were two humans who became exceptions. One was the Baroness von Trapp, of Trapp Family Singers and *Sound of Music* fame, before whom no barrier could stand. The other was a very sexy lady who simply walked in saying. 'Now, don't carry on! After what I've heard of you, I simply had to come and see what you looked like. Yum-yum! What a lovely, great hunk of a man you are! Could I just touch you once or twice?'

Daniel was almost as resentful of the intrusion of animals. Although he was partial to them in other areas, none, except the peacocks, was permitted to enter his sacred places. One day, though, he was overcome by a creature much too large for him to repel either by voice or force. Leaving it in sole possession, he fled the scene and came down to me in a state of acute perturbation.

'There's a bull in my workshop! It's enormous! It came in the back way! I can't drive it out the front door because it wouldn't get through, and if we try to turn it around it will surely knock everything over — maybe scratch some! What shall I do?'

I looked up the slope, and there truly was at least a bull's head looking benignly out from the narrow doorway. The rest was lost in the dimness behind. It was one of two great, polled beasts which were pastured in our front paddock to keep the grass short. To keep themselves from boredom in the one-and-a-half hectare paddock they engaged in tournaments, sometimes ending with one of them forced into the dam, but mostly consisting of throat-straining roaring, pawing the ground, and crashing heads together in earth-shaking combat which could have been mortal had they had the horns to accomplish what they promised. I felt weak with the memory of it. I suggested that if we left the intruder alone it might soon go away to where there was grass.

But, after half-an-hour of waiting, the bull was not only still there, but had sat itself down in the careful, heavy way that such enormous animals do, while knocking one sculpture to the ground as it did so. It had probably never sat on anything so warm as the soft sawdust and shavings of the workshop.

Now in despair, Daniel telephoned to the owner and asked for help, specifying that it must come quietly and without dogs to upset the animal.

Three employees came. They conferred before going cautiously in to bring out what pieces of sculpture they could, and push the heavier things closer to the walls. All the time the bull just sat where it was and chewed, while the men grew braver and braver, and more and more jocose at Daniel's expense.

When they had done all they could do they closed off the front door with a low barrier and poked long poles at the giant to make it get up and go out the back way — all the time being steadily entreated by Daniel, who had visions of the huge pain-crazed creature running amok in the confined space, to please mind its eyes and be careful not to hurt it.

It got up at last, behind first, and backed away from its tormentors, lowering its great head and rumbling menacingly, but still reversing until it was out in the sunshine. There it was undecided as to direction until it caught sight of a herd of heifers being driven down from the hills above. As if by magic it lost its lethargy and became a young, dancing Jove again.

After that we had no strange animals dwelling on our land, and a very definite closing of the back way into the workshop.

Perhaps it was just that, like Tim had been, Daniel was much more of a builder than a destroyer and, as with the bull, the romantic way would have been the easiest. To take down the dining-room wall I probably would have had to play my own trump card by telling him he was welcome, if he so wished, to lock himself in the stables while the destruction was taking place. Then his only disturbance would be when I came to sleep with him at night. For him this was a romantic notion as yet unfulfilled, mostly because of the amount of small wildlife, such as the tiny marsupial mouse we had once seen with a baby in its pouch, who were still pleased to inhabit the warmth of that otherwise reserved zone.

Daniel could, if he wished, only come happily out of hiding when the dining-room had been returned to its original elegant proportion and light, and rid forever of the dank, divisive, dark-spreading kitchen. 'Look', I would have said, showing him again my sketches of the renovations. 'Look here! It's all about light! Imagine the new kitchen, made without one external alteration, and with no need to be forever under electric light in the daytime.

'Think of me, think of us both, in this bright, happy, inspiring place which will call for nothing in the way of decoration because it will be looking directly at its own wide windowsful of orange trees and singing birds!.'

And then I would have seen him laughing, charmed by the picture I had conjured, and heard him saying, 'You really needn't have gone in for so much overkill, you know. Just the fact that it will make you happy is enough, except that I'll hold you to at least one night in the stables.'

Leaving aside such dreaming of what had been and what might have been, I resigned myself once again to being alone responsible for any mistakes in planning.

Until a month before we were originally set to begin what was visually the most important work on the inside of the house, I had no better idea than that, because the original big kitchen was away out in the west wing, with no direct communication, the restored dining-room would still have to house the kitchen, as in so many old farmhouses.

The solution came literally in the space between one footfall and the next. I paused with foot up-lifted, had a vision of what could be done, and turned the grounded leg around in order to step back into the little breakfast room which the National Trust architect thought had once been the serving pantry.

Separated from it by a wall was another room of the same size, with access from the side verandah. It was about two-and-a-half metres square and furnished as a bedroom. In mounting excite-ment I saw not only how this would not be missed from its present use, because we already had plenty of bedrooms, but how the wall between it and the breakfast room could come down to give us kitchen and breakfast room combined.

I ran around and looked at the outside and saw that, even if we had to put a beam across the ceiling where the four-metre high wall now stood, there would be no external alteration necessary. I could see it all, as though it were already finished — sink here, cupboards there, table at the other end, two generous Victorian windows, with no wall in between, together opening on to the glory of the old and new fruit and nut trees.

I danced under them and disturbed the drowsy noonday birds.

Still under the influence of the Idea, which comes from beyond habitual thought, I went almost without intention into my study to make the sketches needed. Soon I found myself making others for use in the uncertain future, showing how Old Kitchen and Main House could be harmlessly and beautifully linked by extending my present plans. After that it would have taken a great deal more self-control than I had, to stop myself from at once ringing the ever-enthusiastic carpenter, Brian, and infecting him with a similar excitement.

So it was that two months before we actually began on the dining-room the new kitchen was finished in every way. It was visually more satisfactory than even I had expected. As well as two windows it had the original doors, now at each end of this larger room. All together these more than adequately fulfilled every promise of myriad birds among laden citrus trees. To add to the general euphoria they also immediately showed nut and fruit trees in full blossom, and opened long perspectives down verandahs in both north and south directions.

Having so successfully demolished a small

double-brick wall it was with greater confidence that, as the year came near its close, we made approach to the once-dreaded destruction of the larger one.

When the day came it seemed to be even more right to do it because of the announcement that the Berlin Wall had that day also begun the process of coming down. Its demolition may have been a more complex task, although enthusiastically attended by a great mass of souvenir hunters as unpaid helpers. It is not known whether anybody kept souvenirs of ours, but we had a few volunteers to make the task easier.

Whatever the state of winter weather over there in Berlin, down here it turned out to be a great day for pulling down walls — mildly warm, bright and windless.

Long before we began, the dining-room was already cleared of furniture, the carpet removed and the floor covered with decorators' canvas. I waited almost breathlessly while a counter-check was made to be sure that no part of the roof was resting anywhere on the doomed structure.

When the last moment of possible reprieve was over, the tool was swung against the thick brick barrier and a jagged glimmer of dusty light heralded the greater breadth of that which was in waiting. In the same instant as the wall cracked, the importance of the occasion when it was erected became apparent to me, and I understood why Daniel would have been reluctant to destroy it.

The building of it must had come as a blessed relief to some harassed wife and mother of several children, footsore and weary from continually moving over the insensitive bricks of the back verandah, and through the unaccommodating space between the dining-room and the old kitchen.

So I crack open not only a wall but an event, a kindness long meditated and carried out at last. I have to remind myself that I have provided a better thing for future wives and mothers before I can resume my elevated mood, though now without self-righteousness.

Outside, on those brick verandahs, the half-dozen of helpers began to manoeuvre their wheelbarrows to take the rubble to the waiting utes. There were plenty of workers for the jobs of sorting out the precious good bricks and stacking them behind the stables for future use, and for loading the rejects and the old mortar onto the utilities to be taken and cascaded onto the driveway. Once dumped, there were other workers to hammer them into pieces acceptable to rubber tyres. It was as smooth an operation as any going on at the other side of the world.

By four o'clock the wall was gone, levelled right to the floor, its many years of interference over, its constituents cast to the four winds. The workers drank tea and went home, leaving me to stand gloating in the wideness of the light which was now able to flood in from the radiant west and highlight the perfect proportions of the room.

I stayed there in the enlarged space for a precious while, revelling in the successful furthering of my plan, sometimes looking through the hole in the outside wall where the distorted window had been and where the sink still stood. The rust-streaked tank had been long ago removed, and every bit of the decay Daniel and I had noted on our first evening of ownership made good. There was nothing now to interrupt the long sweep of lawn past the restored superstructure of the deep old well and right up to the stables.

I went out through that other gap where a door had been introduced at the same time as the wall had been built. I walked along the verandah to open the back and front doors of the long passage, then returned in the same way into the dining-room to open its passage door. There I stood marvelling at having brought together in the house at last the light from the four main points of the compass. It spread life over everything in the way it was meant to do. The dust mites which we had carefully shut in all day went riding up on the beckoning draughts between chimneys and lifted windows, or out through open doorways. I think I blessed every one of them as they went.

The wiping out of all traces of the wall, and the reconnection to its past took longer than either Brian or I had estimated. You can be quite sure that work of this kind always will. The ceiling and walls had to be filled and smoothed into one line, the oven removed from the corner fireplace, the chimney made to serve a new purpose.

There was much removing of bricks and pieces of wood, and of looking into cavities to see if one of the many who had dwelt in the house had been a miser who poked gold away. Daniel used to say it must be somewhere, otherwise why were there so many ghosts? The only secretive place we ever discovered was a spring drawer in a desk whose origins were untraceable, and it yielded nothing but a couple of hundred-year-old grocery accounts. I felt like Jane Austen's Catherine in *Northanger Abbey* when she found the washing bills.

Here, even when we removed the old kitchen sink and cupboards, there was nothing. Our only discoveries were of how badly they had stood the test of time, of what a devastating mess the years of leaking plumbing had made. The inside layer of bricks was damaged to the point of needing total replacement, and the floor boards were almost entirely decayed. The access of air caused the smell I had so often commented upon to become an intolerable stink.

We were also compelled to notice that floor damage did not stop at the now exposed edge of the linoleum which we had laid down some ten years earlier. Even as Brian wondered aloud how far the rot had spread up the skirting boards, and if it had damaged the wall as well, I was beginning to realize how the alteration of my original plan for the dining-room, which would have left the floor covering of this part intact, had led me into what could be an agonizing situation.

'Seeing that we've got the bricklayer coming on Wednesday to fix the chimney and fill in the doorway, we'd better get all this flooring up, too', Brian was saying. 'Especially as we may need to find some whole pieces of old skirting — though I don't give much for the chances. Is that all right with you?'

It was hard to make any sort of answer. I was back in that older time with Tim and Daniel. We were all standing together, surveying those same skirting boards and hoping that everything was as dry as the rest of the foundations had proved to be. The whole of the following sequence, right down to the placing of the gifts beside the bones, became so present, the characters so alive, that all I could do was to mutter some sort of excuse to Brian, and take the tableaux out of the room with me.

It was not long before guilt came rushing to engulf me, saying that of the three who had knelt beside the fatal place and there agreed that the knowledge of the remains of the young woman should remain secret, I would naturally be the one who was at last to be the betrayer. It was probable that the investigation of the floorboards would lead Brian, at least out of curiosity, to open up the manhole. That would inevitably lead to the violation against which Daniel and I had so passionately spoken.

If you had not gone away, I told him reproachfully, we could have made sure it did not happen. But I knew that the fault was all my own, caused by my fixation with enabling light to return to dark places, wanting to make them again as perfect in form and atmosphere as when they were conceived.

The thought of what was to happen was so abhorrent to me that it was some time before I could return to answer the carpenter. I had resolved that I must be very casual about it, to be careful not to show any symptom of anxiety. Could it be that I could use my authority to keep the square in place?

When I came back into the room, Brian had already removed a quantity of the skirting board, which was damp in places, but not decayed. But underneath it the render on the lower part of the wall was running down like loose sand. I remembered that after we had found the bones we had not gone further into investigations of damp.

Brian stood up. 'So far not bad, but I think I'll leave this until tomorrow, if you don't mind. I've just remembered I've got to take my wife shopping, and she hates to be hurried over it. But I'll tear all the floor covering up in the morning, and I promise you we'll have a good look at everything.'

He wasn't out of the drive before I had the mad idea of myself pulling up the flooring under which the secret — which was now my sole responsibility — lay waiting to be a secret no longer. I thought of removing the bones and putting all back again. It did not take long for reason to see that even the first part of such a job would be impossible for an unskilled person to carry out with the minimum tools available, and without doing irreparable damage to even the first part — the removal of the precious and possibly irreplaceable thirty centimetre high ornamental skirting boards. After that would come the cutting into the wallboard covering the flooring boards — impossible once again with the tools I had, and my lack of skill in using them. Then to free the manhole with the long, grooved, handmade nails which I had seen Tim drive in on the angle. All impossible! Every bit of it. And also impossible to explain any of it to Brian in the morning.

I knew then, though I desperately tried to find some way out of it, that I must either exert myself as owner to keep the manhole closed, and maybe set gossip going, or let Brian open it and throw myself on his mercy. I was fairly sure, because his integrity and his respect for Daniel were as Tim's had ever been, that he would consent to the secrecy which Daniel, as well as myself, had thought to be right.

Thus I strove to reassure myself, hour after hour, through the long night of no longer knowing whether my restoration work was of any merit at all in the light of what was about to happen. None of it would stand up for an instant against the misery consequent on the ensuing publicity if the finding of the bones was made known along with the evidence of our earlier involvement.

I thought of Adam and his instinctive knowledge — his great cry that he could no longer walk with his boots over the wrongs the white man had done to his people — Adam whom I had once betrayed to the police! Now I could see it as nothing else. What would he think if he should ever know of this coming betrayal, not only of the grave of one of his people, but of Daniel's wish — made clearly manifest by the carving lying beside her pitiful skeleton — to let the girl remain in undisputed possession of her own grave?

It was a long night of almost constant

movement of mind and body, of going to bed and getting up out of its intolerable stillness to walk around the house, to mooch about outside in the light of the moon, to ascend the stair to the attic studio and review it all again amongst the sculptures, and come back to bed to find the same questions surfacing again and again; all the time knowing that whatever I did, short of suicide, the interminable night would not be long enough to avoid the coming events and bring me peace.

Brian came early. I watched his wiry, compact figure unpacking the tools which were so dear to him that he took them away in their entirety every evening, and I wondered how such a well-known and welcome person could have assumed, in so short a while, the character of a nemesis.

He seemed to be even hastening towards it. He took the skirting off in almost no time, and the rendering crumbled off the wall in just the same way as it had done the evening before. The strips of tin at the bottom of the boards had evidently been placed there because of the deterioration. He took up the electric saw to cut the glued-down floor covering into sections, so as to lift it, as he did so saying, 'I'm afraid we shall have to replace a board or two along here. It may be damp from some cause other than the leaking sink. We'll have to find out what.'

My heart seemed to hit rock bottom. I said

weakly, excluding Tim because the decisions had been taken by Daniel and myself, 'You won't need to go underneath, Brian. Daniel and I looked down there, and there was nothing bad.'

He grinned at me, knowingly. 'Well, that's good; but Daniel looking with half of him wanting to get back to his own work, and me looking when it's my job to do so, are two very different things. He didn't even bother to remove the skirtings, did he?' That was when I knew nothing would save me.

I stood there numbly and dumbly until something of my anxiety must have communicated itself. 'Look', he said, 'if it's paying me you're so worried about — ?'

'No, no! I — I was just thinking about Daniel, that's all.' I could see I had embarrassed him. He sighed. 'Yes, Daniel. How he would have loved this — now it's nearly finished, of course. And old Tim, too. He cared so much that the place should be made good again — mostly because Daniel wanted it, I guess. You know, when I'm working here, like now, I can often feel Tim close by, as well as Daniel.'

I felt like saying, Yes, they're right beside you; they're all around us, all of those others, too, every one who ever was here, all watching for what I will do. But I couldn't make words come. I went through the doorway to the kitchen and filled the kettle for morning tea while I tried to tell myself none of it mattered unless I made it do so; and that whatever Brian and I were going to see might really have been happening light years ago, and was only now becoming visible to our sight. I was surprised to see that my hands were not shaking like the heart in my breast.

Brian was just getting up the last of the wall-board as I went towards him. He looked around. 'Look at this!' he said. 'There's a manhole here! Isn't that good?'

While he went over to get a torch and pick up a screwdriver to lever up the lid, I just stood there trying to find future words. Any arrangement of speech was shocked out of me when it came up easily. There were no long, handmade nails holding it down!

As if I were back in that earlier time I moved over beside the kneeling tradesman and looked down as he switched the torch on.

There was nothing there!

That is, there was nothing but a few curved lines, as though a hand had smoothed over disturbed dry earth, and showing very faintly beneath the sprinkling of dust that must have fallen from underneath the floorboards during the late cataclysm, were two handprints.

One I knew better than the other. It was a small hand for a man, and it was the artistic hand of

Daniel. The other was the lovely long, narrow hand-print typical of very many Aboriginal people, and it could only have belonged to Adam.

From somewhere away out, there came towards me an intense, interminable ray of musical light, like no other music and no other light I have ever known. When it finally reached me I began to understand at last.

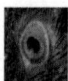

CHAPTER TWELVE

Freedom

'WHAT A PLACE! WHAT builders they were! It's all as dry as a bone down there', cried Brian. 'And the floorboards are all OK here, too. When the bricklayer has repaired the other damage we can put the skirtings back and forget it. Now, isn't that just great? Nothing more for either you or the house to worry about, ever.'

Too full of dawning realization for any speech, I could only nod my head and smile at him. I went outside and walked across the courtyard with the light still in and around me, loving with all my heart the openness of everything.

A flight of ibis became visible travelling in from the east. They wheeled above me, making a halo against the sky, revealing themselves as of the straw-necked kind before gliding down to settle on the small dam. I had never seen so many before. Usually they were alone, or in pairs.

When they were standing in the water, looking in admiration at their own reflections, I sat myself down on a log with my back to the bole of the giant elm tree. It was one of the old vantage points from which the peacocks had delighted to watch Daniel at work, and it was liberally spattered with peacock droppings.

Looking out from the leaf-patterned light into the clear day, I let the wider light of my recent understanding crystalize memory into words.

I saw Daniel and myself, radiant with pleasure that I was home from the Centre, and surrounded by the golden glow of the winter sun sinking behind our hills. I saw again the peacocks, gold-illumed as from an old manuscript, jumping down to display their joy in existing with us as creatures of that sun.

I remembered the unity of every thing about us, and out of it Daniel telling me of Adam's visit, and their mutual rapport. Of how, up there in the hills on the third day, they had made a ceremony. It was a ritual, as authentic as thousands of years could make it, and carried out as the inheritors of the origi-nal people would have wished. It was a ceremony which included the burying of the wrongs which took place here, on this property. It purified Jinwirringee and made it free of them for ever. 'Gillian, it was so great, so wonderful... I can't tell you here and now how wonderful. I must have you up there with me in the higher hills ... the thing is so big for both of us, so important that it needs the mountains to help me to put it into your mind. Can you wait a few days while I catch up with my work?'

Daniel! The Daniel with whom I had in the last short space of one decade watched an aurora australis, a comet and a supernova moving with innumerable stars in endless space. I had watched many things with Daniel, a man overwhelmed with wonder yet never shaken in his belief in the validity of his own contribution!

So the days had become weeks by the time he decided, minutes before his death and with that work as finished as his mortal hands would make it, that it was at last the day to lead me into the high hills and pass on to me what Adam had given to him. And he to Adam. And both of them to the lass who had lain so long under the floorboards. And all of them to me.

Adam! Adam, the outcast, warned away from every state in the country! He who had come to us with dew on his rumpled clothes, twigs in his hair, and nothing of his own, had combined with Daniel to give my small Aboriginal friend, Jinwirringee and myself, full freedom from the punishing past.

I knew then that our Australian identity is not complete without having its base firmly established on the fact of its original culture being not European, but Aboriginal.

I left the shelter of the tree and walked away. I

walked up past the big dam and the spring and through a herd of grazing cattle, following the densely-wooded ridge up to a clearing on top of the hill. Here I could see clearly the higher range behind. Somewhere in the vastness over there two men had performed the rites of burial.

I wondered if they had stripped naked and coloured themselves for perfect equality and so they could merge into the landscape without difference or pretence? I could vision their figures walking with ritual steps, carrying the light weight of the anonymous but important bones, and the heavy one of humanities' racial prejudices.

I could see them look together over the land which the invading pastoralists had so much changed, and then once at each other, agreeing on that acceptance which allows us to begin new freedoms, before they laid their burdens down where the forgiving earth would make everything one.

As l came down, I began to realize the extent of the freedom I had gained. I knew that the compulsive drive to repay something indefinable, which had been mine for a dozen years, was gone from me forever. What little was left to be done would now be the absolute gift of one who was free to choose. I could stay, or I could go.

Walking down the cool groin of the hills towards the meeting of the rivers I was so sensuously at home with the earth that I would willingly have dissolved into it. Suddenly, as I emerged from the deep bush, there were great birds about me, apparent to me in the same way as those others which had come years before with Daniel's words. But these were not peacocks. I saw them clearly as lyrebirds; birds in shape reminiscent of the history of the world's musical aspiration and invention; birds with limitless resonances, able to enjoy and give back the voices of others; birds utterly in harmony with the land.

And never to go away.